THE LOST LANGUAGE

The lines spoken in the play are quoted from
Lewis Carroll's *Alice in Wonderland* and
Through the Looking Glass.

Margaret Ferguson Books
Copyright © 2021 by Claudia Mills
All Rights Reserved
HOLIDAY HOUSE is registered in the U.S. Patent and Trademark Office.
Printed and bound in August 2021 at Maple Press, York, PA, USA.
www.holidayhouse.com
First Edition

1 3 5 7 9 10 8 6 4 2

Library of Congress Cataloging-in-Publication Data
Names: Mills, Claudia, author.
Title: The lost language / by Claudia Mills.
Description: First edition. | New York : Holiday House, [2021]
"A Margaret Ferguson Book." | Audience: Ages 9 to 12.
Audience: Grades 4–6. | Summary: Best friends and sixth-graders
Bumble and Lizard go on a quest to save the severely endangered language,
Guernésiais, partly to impress Bumble's linguist mother.
Identifiers: LCCN 2020043807 | ISBN 9780823450381 (hardcover)
Subjects: CYAC: Best friends—Fiction. | Friendship—Fiction.
Middle schools—Fiction. | Schools—Fiction. | Language and
languages—Fiction. | Family life—Fiction.
Classification: LCC PZ7.M63963 Lp 2021 | DDC [Fic]—dc23
LC record available at https://lccn.loc.gov/2020043807

ISBN: 978-0-8234-5038-1(hardcover)

THE LOST LANGUAGE

Claudia Mills

MARGARET FERGUSON BOOKS
HOLIDAY HOUSE · NEW YORK

To Lisa Rowe Fraustino, Susan Campbell Bartoletti, and

Molly Fisk,

who helped me rediscover

the language of poetry

THE LOST LANGUAGE

Things I've Lost: A Partial List

Pooh Bear.
I took him on vacation
and he got left behind in the hotel bed,
but my dad called and two days later
a lumpy package arrived in the mail,
and the lump was Pooh.

My jacket on the bus
for the class trip to the planetarium.
Well, I almost lost it,
but Lizard noticed in the nick of time
and raced back to our seat
and grabbed it for me.

My special lucky button,
when I had a hole in my pants pocket.
Lizard found that for me, too.

My glasses, in Buddha Delight,
when my mother had already said
she couldn't handle One More Thing,
and I knew that losing my glasses
would have counted as One More Thing,
but I told my dad, and he took care of it
and my mother never had to know,
so whew for that.

Pencils.

More pencils.

You may have noticed that I got
everything back again,
except the pencils,
but everyone loses pencils,
and anyway the world is full of pencils.

You also may have noticed that it's always
other people who get the lost things back for me.

So what would happen if you lost those people?
Who would help you get them back again?

Two Girls Named Elizabeth

Lizard's name isn't really Lizard.
(You probably already knew that.)
But here's the strange thing. My best friend
and I both have the same name: Elizabeth.
Only she was Liz, and I was Betsy.

(Here's another strange thing:
How can *Betsy* be a nickname for *Elizabeth*?)

But when we started being best friends
in third grade, she said Betsy
was a dumb name and I should be Liz, too.

So for one week, we were both Liz,
which made us the *best* best friends ever.

Except that it was confusing.

So she said she'd change her name to Lizard,
and I'd be the only Liz, but I said,
in a very small voice, that I'd rather be
the only Betsy, and she gave a big sigh,
and said she'd call me B (for Betsy),
and then it became Bumblebee,
and then it was just Bumble.

Now we're in sixth grade, and she's Lizard
to everyone in the world,
even to her parents and her sisters,

even to teachers who sometimes forget that Lizard
isn't a name teachers should be calling anyone.

And I'm Bumble to her,
but not to anyone else.

So when we're together,
just the two of us,
we become two girls
named Lizard and Bumble.

What My Mom Thinks of the Name Bumble

She hates it.

The first time she heard
Lizard say, "Bye, Bumble!"

my mom said, "*Bumble?*"
And Lizard said, "That's her nickname."

My mom said, "Her nickname is *Betsy*."
And Lizard said, "Bumble is *my* nickname for her."

My mom said, "*Bumble*, as in *blunder*?
Bumble, as in *stumble*? *Bumble*, as in *fumble*?

Bumble, as *move in an awkward way*?
Bumble, as *speak in a confused way*?"

My mom knows more about words
than anybody I know.

"*Bumble* like *bumblebee*," Lizard said.
"Bumblebees buzzing around beautiful flowers."

I could tell my mom wanted to tell Lizard not to call me that,
but she didn't want to be mean to my new best friend.

But every time my mom hears Lizard call me Bumble,
which has been a *lot* of times over the last three years,

I can see her jaw tighten
with all the things she isn't saying.

Movers and Shakers

My mother says Lizard
is a mover and shaker.
She didn't say,
but I know she means,
I'm the one
who is
moved and shaken.

Like This One Time

Lizard was at my house,
sorting little pieces of broken tile
that my father brought from his workshop
to glue onto cheap plastic plates
to turn them into mosaic platters
for a banquet she and I were going to have.

Not a banquet for lots of people,
with roasted pheasant and cups of mead,
like in the book about the Middle Ages
we had just read together.
Just a banquet for the two of us,
with oatmeal raisin cookies and grape juice.

I was picking out some blue and silver
pieces for mine,
but Lizard said we should both make ours
with red and gold.
So I started to put the blue and silver
pieces away.

My mother was helping to cover the kitchen table
with newspaper so we wouldn't get glue on it,
and she said to Lizard,
"Why don't *you* make *yours* the way *you* want.
And *Betsy* can make *hers* the way *she* wants."

"Sure," Lizard said.
Then she added under her breath,
"If Bumble doesn't care that no kings and queens
would ever have *silver* platters if they could have *gold*,
and red goes with gold better than blue does."

So I made mine red and gold, too.

And I couldn't tell if my mother was more mad at Lizard
for telling me what to do,

or more disappointed in me
for doing it.

Lizard Can Stand Up to Anybody

Lizard stands up to teachers,
like when she told Mrs. Henderson
that Columbus didn't *discover* America
because America had already been discovered
thousands of years earlier
by the people who were already living there
when Columbus showed up with his ships.

She stands up to bullies,
like when she saw some bigger boys
throwing a stone at a bunny
and told them she was going to report them to the SPCA,
which she said was the abbreviation for
the Society for the Prevention of Cruelty to Animals,
and they said, "Yeah, right. Go ahead and report us."
But they dropped their stones and walked away.

She stood up to Clarence Keaton,
who sat behind me in third grade and pulled my braids,
not in a friendly playful way, but hard.
She told him, "A boy pulled Bumble's braids last year,
and I told on him, and he ended up going to jail,"
which was completely not true,
because we didn't even know each other in second grade.
And no one would put a second-grade kid
in jail for pulling someone's hair.
They'd probably get in-school suspension.
But Clarence never pulled my braids again.

It is a very useful thing sometimes
to be best friends
with the bravest girl in the school.

Things I'm Afraid Of

Shots at the doctor,
though mainly just the minute before the shot
when I see the nurse coming toward me
with the needle.

Getting tests back
when the teacher hands it to me facedown.

Scary music in a movie
when the movie is already scary enough
that I don't need creepy tones to make it scarier.

Dogs that have rabies.

Dogs that don't have rabies
but might bite me anyway.

My mother when she's stressed.

Loud noises.

Worms on the sidewalk after it rains.

Mushrooms that sprout up on the lawn after it rains.

Lizard sometimes,
when she gets that glint in her eyes
like she's going to talk me into doing something
I'm going to be sorry for afterward.

Lizard sometimes,
how mad she might get
if I didn't let her talk me into things
I didn't want to be sorry for afterward.

Having everybody,
especially Lizard and my mother,
think I'm a fraidy-cat.

Things Lizard Is Afraid Of

Nothing.

Lizard (and Me) at School

We were both in Mrs. Henderson's class
in third grade.

Sometimes I wonder how different my life would be
if the person at Sandrock Elementary who decides which kids
to put in each class hadn't put me and Lizard together.

Who *is* that person? Is it the principal?
Or the school secretary? Does a computer do the picking?

Or is it Fate, which Lizard says doesn't exist,
but I think maybe does.

Why else would two girls named Elizabeth
both have braids with blue ribbons on the first day?

My braids were the color people call dishwater blond.
Hers were black like a night with no moon and no stars.

"I hate braids," Lizard said
(only she wasn't Lizard yet).
"I think they look dumb. I'm taking mine out."
And then Lizard didn't have braids anymore.

I loved my braids, but I said,
"I think they look dumb, too."
But I didn't take mine out.
My mother wouldn't like it
if I came home without them
after she had gone to so much trouble
to put them in.

"Yours don't look as dumb as mine," Lizard said.

That's when I started liking Lizard.
And I think that's when she started liking me.

The Next Year

Lizard and I weren't in the same class in fourth grade.
I have a feeling my mother said something to somebody
to make that happen.

"I think this is going to be the year you really bloom,"
my mother said.

"I'm excited to see what new friends you'll make,"
my mother said.

"It'll be good for you and Lizard to have your own space,"
my mother said.

"Friends don't have to be joined at the hip, you know,"
my mother said.

I didn't say anything.

I didn't want to bloom that year
if blooming meant not being friends with Lizard anymore.

The only friend I wanted was Lizard.

The only space I needed was the space where Lizard was.

Even if we weren't joined at the hip,
Lizard and I were joined at the heart.

P.S. About Fourth Grade

Lizard and I still saw each other
all the time.
And I didn't bloom.
Or if I did, nobody noticed,
including me.

The Year after That

Lizard and I were together again in fifth grade.
I have a feeling Lizard's mother said something to somebody
to make that happen.

"My mother thinks you're a good influence on me," Lizard said.
Then she laughed. I laughed, too.

As if I could ever influence Lizard about anything.

Sixth Grade

Now we're at Southern Peaks Middle School.
School just started,
and we have three classes apart:
language arts, social studies, and our "specials"—
band for Lizard and art for me.
But we have three classes together:
science, math, PE.
Plus lunch. Hooray!

I don't think anybody's mother
said anything to anybody
to make this happen.

In middle school Fate—
or the computer—
has a lot more power
than parents do.

Other Friends

Lizard and I have friends
besides each other.

But not a lot.
And not close friends.

Lizard has to be the first at everything.
Most kids aren't as good as I am at being second.

That sounds strange: being good at being second.
But I think it's a talent, sort of,

not to mind things other people mind.
I truly don't mind if I say, "Let's watch TV

without the sound on and make up the words,"
and Lizard says, "That's boring,"

even though she's the one who first thought up
doing it, so who is she to say

it's boring now that it's my favorite thing?
(Well, maybe I do mind this a little bit.)

But mostly I don't care that much what we do,
so long as we do it together.

My Mother

My mother can speak five languages fluently:
English (duh), French, Italian, German, and Russian.
That's her job—to know stuff about languages.

She's a professor of linguistics at the university,
and even though she already speaks
more languages than anyone I know,
she studies other languages
that hardly anyone speaks anymore.

She travels to the places where very old people live
who still speak those languages.
The last people to speak a language
are always old,
because as the world becomes
more and more connected,
young people are the first
to learn new ways of living
and new ways of speaking.

So my mother tries to learn
as much of each dying language as she can:
the words in it,
and the rules for how to put the words together.

She records the old people talking
and writes a book about each language
so that when the language is finally lost and forgotten,
there will be at least someone
in the world
who made it possible
to remember.

What Other People's Parents Do

Lizard says her dad is a spy,
but that can't be true.

Her mom works in an office somewhere.

Zari's dad does stuff on his computer.
Her mom is some kind of medical person.

Zoey's dad came to school in first grade
to talk about being a pilot.

Zoey's mom is a stay-at-home mom.
I think she does some catering, too.

Veronica's parents have a hardware store,
but I've never been there.

A lot of kids know my dad makes furniture
because he was interviewed on the local news once,

and the furniture he makes is so beautiful.
People know my mom is a professor,

but I'm not sure they know what she teaches.
It's not the kind of thing kids talk about.

I think parents talk about us
a lot more than we talk about them.

How My Father Met My Mother

They were both graduate students at the same university.

She was studying linguistics
because she already knew she wanted to spend her life
learning all the amazing ways humans talk to one another.

He was studying business
because he couldn't find a job with his philosophy degree,
and his father said, "I'll pay for two more years of school
if you study something *useful* this time."

The coffee shop where he was studying was crowded,
so he invited her to share his table.

"And then we started talking instead of studying,"
he says whenever he tells the story,
which is often.
"And I was in love after ten minutes.
She made me want to find something to do with my life
that would make my eyes shine the way hers did
when she talked about the grammar of the Urdu language.
She made me want to find something to do with my life
that would make my hands move as fast as hers,
like hummingbirds at a feeder full of nectar,
when she talked about how many languages
people speak in Papua New Guinea.

But then I realized I already knew deep inside
that what I loved was woodworking.
So I apologized for wasting my dad's money,
dropped out of business school,
and apprenticed myself to a cabinetmaker.

Now I have work I love,
and the woman I love,
and the daughter I love."
(He always puts in the part about me.)

"So you could say that I'm pretty much
the luckiest guy in the world."

Givers and Takers

Lizard says that
givers always marry takers.
Takers can't marry takers
because they'd both want to do the taking.
Givers could marry givers
except the takers are so good at taking
they get there first.

Lizard's mother is a giver,
according to Lizard,
and her father is a taker.
My father is a giver,
according to Lizard,
and my mother is a taker.

It's true my father is a giver,
but it's not exactly true
my mother is a taker.
Or at least I don't think she means to be.
It's more that she has to give
all the time to everyone else:
her students who take the exams she has to grade
and then come to her to complain if they get a B,
and the other professors in her department,
who pressure her to be on
all the time-consuming committees
they don't want to be on.
But mostly she tries to give to the people
whose languages are dying so fast

that even if she worked every minute of every day,
which she practically does already,
she couldn't learn about them in time.

So she doesn't have a lot
of giving left over
for my father
and me.

I'm Going to Say a Terrible Thing

I sort of like it best when my mother travels
to a faraway part of the world
and spends a whole month sometimes
learning other people's languages all day long.

My mother is usually the one who does the cooking,
which is strange because she's also the one who is crazy-busy,
but she says cooking keeps her sane.
She makes elegant meals
we eat by candlelight,
because elegant meals by candlelight
make her feel calmer and less stressed.

When she's away, my father and I find recipes
in a cookbook that tells you how to make the food
the characters eat in famous children's books.
Afterward we don't clean up the kitchen
because there is no one here but us and maybe Lizard,
who doesn't mind sticky counters
or burnt sauce on the stove.

I can practice piano as much or as little
as I want, and it's strange,
but I actually end up practicing more.

We don't have to think about
whether my mother had a bad day at the university
because George Bixler said that linguistic fieldwork
(which is what my mother does)
isn't as intellectually rigorous as theoretical linguistics
(which is what he does).

We don't have to see how pale and drawn she looks
after staying up till three o'clock
trying to finish another chapter
of the book she's writing
about one of the dying languages.

And Lizard says,
"I wish I lived at your house,"
which she never says
when my mother is here.

But I Still Love When My Mom Comes Home Again

My dad and I go to the airport and wait
where the international arrivals come in,
and she doesn't come, and she doesn't come,
and suddenly there she is, looking like a stranger,
but also exactly like my mom.

Her face, crinkled and worn
from a super-long flight,
lights up like the twinkle lights
my dad keeps on the backyard deck all year.

She hugs me so tight
while my father hugs her.
"I missed you!
God, how I missed you!"
she says over and over again,
and I love her right then
more than anyone else in the world,
even my father,
even Lizard,
and I wish I could
keep her twinkle lights sparkling
every single day.

But I can't.

Lizard's Superpower

Lizard always knows everything first.
Maybe it's because she has two older sisters,

or her father really is a spy and tells her things
he learns from spying. She was the first to know

Aiden A. had lice and Eloise's parents were
getting divorced. She knew about the divorce

even before Eloise did. She knew Tad would
be elected class president even though everyone

said they had voted for Singh and Rok. Even
things about the world, she knows them first.

She's the one who told me, way back in third grade,
that the polar ice caps are melting and whole

countries will be covered with water someday.
She told me most eggs come from chickens who live

squished together in tiny cages that make the chickens
so frantic that the farmers have to cut off their beaks

so they won't peck each other to death.
Lizard's favorite things to know first are bad things.

Sometimes I think she loves knowing bad things first
just so she can be the one to roll her eyes

at everyone else—especially me—and say,
"I thought *everybody* knew *that*."

I think a little part of her also likes how sad
I feel when the things I thought were true

turn out
not to be.

The One Time I Know Something First

Today, Monday,
when we're at Lizard's house after school,
Lizard tells me that a third of all animal species
might go extinct because of global climate change.

I say, "Did you know that thousands
of languages are going extinct, too?"

I expect her to say, "*Everybody* knows *that*."
But instead she says, "*Languages* can't go extinct."

I say, "Yes, they can." And I tell her about my mom
and the dying languages she writes books about.

"I thought your mom was an anthropologist," she says,
making it sound like she knows more about my mom than I do.

"She's not. She's a linguist," I reply. And Lizard says,
in this accusing kind of way, "I'm sure you said

she was an anthropologist," as if I wouldn't know
my own mother's job! But I know she is just mad

that I broke the rule that I'm supposed to be the one
who knows things second. I didn't even realize

it was a rule until then,
when I broke it.

Why I Love Lizard Anyway

You might wonder why I would be best friends
with someone who always acts like we're playing school
and every single time she gets to be the teacher.

But then Lizard says—and this is why I love Lizard anyway—
"What if rather than *writing* about dying languages,
like your mom, you and I *saved* one instead?"

Lizard's Hobby Is Saving Things

I shouldn't have been surprised that
Lizard wanted to save a dying language.

Once in fifth grade
Lizard found a bird that was attacked
by the neighbor's cat,
and she made her mother take it to
the Wild Bird Rehabilitation Center,
even though her mother said,
"Lizard, it's a bird. Birds die all the time."
Lizard said, "Not *this* bird."

And guess who lived?
Yes, that would be the bird.

And remember that bunny
Lizard saved from the stone-throwing boys?

And remember how Lizard saved me
from braid-pulling Clarence Keaton?

Saving things is Lizard's hobby.

Lizard's Plan

Of course, Lizard being Lizard,
she has a plan.

Of course, Bumble being Bumble,
I'm supposed to carry it out.

"Ask your mom what would be the best
language for us to start saving!

And she can teach it to us
so that we can speak it to each other!

The more we learn of it,
the more of it we'll be saving!"

"That's a good plan," I tell Lizard.
"It totally is."

But I'm not sure
I totally believe it.

My Doubts

I ask Lizard,
"But even if you and I learn how to speak
some dying language,
how is this going to *save* it?"

Lizard flings up her hands
as if this is too obvious for her to have to explain.

"A language dies if *nobody* speaks it!
So it can't be totally dead,
like dead-dead-dead,
if there is still *somebody* in the world
who speaks it, right?

And *we're* somebody!
We're *two* somebodies!

Once your mom teaches us,
we can teach other people at school,
and maybe half the kids at Southern Peaks
will speak the language after a few months.
Think how many somebodies that will be!"

The Biggest Problem of All

But then I say,
"I'm just not sure. . . . I don't think . . .

I mean, I can't see my mother having
time to give us language lessons.

She teaches all day at the university,
so she isn't going to want to do extra teaching

when she gets home at night. She's already
a year behind on writing her current book.

Plus, right now she's incredibly stressed
from waiting to hear if she got the big grant

she needs for her next trip.
Grants are what pay for the research

she does to study the dying languages.
Studying dying languages is so much work!

It's so much work even to get the money
she needs to do the work!

So I just don't see how
we could ask her

to take on
One More Thing."

What I Don't Tell Lizard

Besides, you know she doesn't like
that you call me Bumble
and boss me around
and have to be the know-it-all
all the time about everything.

She isn't going to want to spend her time,
not that she has any time,
but if she did have any time,
she isn't going to want to spend it
carrying out a Lizard Plan.

She just isn't.

Lizard Clearly Isn't Going to Let This Drop

"But don't you see? We'll be *helping* your mom!

It'll be like the three of us
are a language-saving *team*.

She'll be *grateful* to us.
Bumble, your mom is a lonely hero!

She's fighting a brave
battle all by herself.

Think how much *less* tired and stressed she'd be
if two amazing kids were fighting with her!"

Maybe Lizard Does Know the Part I Didn't Say about How My Mother Feels about Her

"In fact, I bet,"
Lizard adds,
"when she finds out what you and I
are doing to save our language,
she's going to tell you,
Dearest daughter, I was wrong about Lizard.
It was the luckiest day of my life
when you and Lizard became best friends."

I'm Still Not Convinced

"Do we have to learn the whole language?"
I ask Lizard.

"Of course not!
Nobody knows a *whole* language!
Not even your mom.

Millions and millions of people
speak English,
but nobody on earth knows
every single word
in the entire English language.

Everybody on earth
only knows
part of a language.

Nobody ever knows
the *whole*
of anything."

My Brilliant Idea

"I have an idea," I tell Lizard.
"We don't need my mom
to help us.

Why don't we learn
as much of the language as we can,
just the two of us?

We can keep it a secret
for as long as we can
and save as much of it as we can.

And then it will be
a surprise gift for my mom:
'Ta-da! Look what we did!'"

I hold my breath.
Then Lizard gives a huge grin
and says "Yes!"

What I Admit to Myself (but Not to Lizard)

I'm not sure I can
see any of this actually happening.

Will Lizard and I really learn
how to speak a dying language?

Will we really teach other kids
how to speak it, too?

But it's more likely to happen
than my being able to talk my mother

into being a language-saving team
with me and Lizard.

And . . .
maybe . . .

this *could* happen.
Maybe it *will* happen?

Maybe my mother will
finally like my best friend?

Maybe my mother will
be proud of me, too?

The World Is Very Big

That's the first thing Lizard and I learn
when we sit down at her family's computer on Tuesday
and Google "endangered languages."

I mean, we knew the world was big,
but it looks bigger when we find a website
that has a map of every single country on earth
with thousands of colored dots all over it
for thousands of "endangered languages."
How are we going to pick which one to save?

Have I Mentioned I Hate Picking Things?

Like ordering food in restaurants, where I know
that whatever I choose, when the food comes,
the other person's food is going to look better.

Or what to wear on the first day of school.

Or which presents to give people.

It's easy to pick for my father because he likes
everything, or at least he's good at pretending.
Or maybe he truly does like everything
so long as it comes from me.

It's hard for my mother because she doesn't like
anything and she tries to pretend.
But there're these little lines at the side
of her mouth that give her away.

Last Christmas I found these cute
ceramic mice holding signs that said
World's Best Father
and World's Best Mother.

They weren't Disney-type mice,
which I knew my mother wouldn't like,
because she hates anything to do with Disney.
They were Beatrix Potter–type mice,
and my mother used to read me Beatrix Potter
stories all the time when I was little.

My father hugged me and said,
"Now I need to find a mouse that says
World's Best Daughter."

"World's Best," my mother said,
and she sounded sad, like she already knew
she wasn't the World's Best Mother,
and maybe she already knew I wasn't
the World's Best Daughter, either.

How Do We Pick?

"Okay," Lizard says. "Here's how we'll do it."
Sometimes it's a relief to have a best friend who's bossy.

"The map says that the orange dots are for *endangered*,
and the red dots are for *severely endangered*.

We want *severely endangered*
because they need saving more.

Then we pick a continent.
Not North America,

because we already live there,
and that would be boring

(even though there are dozens
of red dots right here in the United States!).

Then we pick a country.
Let's pick one we've never heard of.
Oh, and it has to be a language
where someone like your mother

already made a list of the words we need to learn.
Otherwise how can we learn them?"

I look on the website
at the list of countries
that have endangered languages.

I haven't heard of most of them.
Azerbaijan. Belarus. Brunei.
Burkina Faso. Caledonia. East Timor.

Gambia. Guinea-Bissau. Kiribati.
Kyrgyzstan. New Caledonia.

Niue. Oman. Pitcairn. Suriname.
This is already impossible.

Lizard Picks for Us (of Course)

Then Lizard clicks a few more keys on the computer
and points to the screen where it says "Guernésiais."

"Red dot for *severely endangered*."
She clicks a few more times
to Google a few more things.
"And there's some language guides right here online."

But . . . but . . . but . . .

What about the other severely endangered languages?
There's a whole huge world filled
with desperate little red dots.

For the first time I understand
why my mother feels completely
overwhelmed all the time.

Lizard looks over at me expectantly,
so I say the thing she expects me to say.

"Great!"

We could spend the rest of our lives
picking which red dot to save
and not saving any.

Or we could just decide:
"Let's save this one."

A Dot on a Dot

The language Lizard picked
is called Guernésiais.
I don't know how to pronounce that.
But if we are going to speak this language
we have to at least be able to say its name.

Lizard looks that up, too.
"It's JERR-nehz-yay."

"JERR-nehz-yay,"
I echo.

It's the language people speak—
well, used to speak—
on a little island called Guernsey
in the English Channel
between France and England.

The red dot for *severely endangered*
practically covers up
the dot on the map for Guernsey.

I like that we're going to save
a dot on a dot.

A dot on a dot
seems even more in need of saving.

Two Hundred Plus Two

The website says only two hundred people
still speak Guernésiais.

After Lizard and I start speaking it,
then it will be two hundred plus two.

Will that make a big enough difference
to count as helping to save a language?

When Lizard saved the bird,
she knew the bird was saved
when she and her mother got a call
from the bird rehab place
and went to watch them release it
and saw it fly away.
How will we know
when we've done enough
to save Guernésiais?

Lizard must be thinking the same thing.

"*We're* just two people," she says,
"but, remember, if we get everyone
at Southern Peaks Middle School
to start speaking it,
that will be four hundred more people.
That's *double* the number of people."

I try to imagine everyone at Southern Peaks
starting to speak Guernésiais.

This is not that easy to imagine.

But if anyone can make that happen,
it's Lizard.

How to Say Hello on Our Dot

"*Baonjour*," Lizard says to me.
"*Baonjour*," I reply.

It sounds sort of like *hello* in French.
I know some French because my mother signed me up
for an after-school French class once.
She let me quit after she found out
the teacher had a bad accent.

When I tell this to Lizard,
she does this Lizard thing
where her eyes flash
and her nostrils flare
and her lips get pressed
tight together.

I can tell she thinks
maybe we picked the wrong language.

She doesn't want to save a language
that sounds too much like another language.
She wants to save a language
that doesn't sound like anything else
in the whole entire world.

"I said it sounds *sort* of like *hello* in French,"
I say right away.
"A lot of languages sound *sort* of like other languages.
Probably every language sounds *sort* of like something else."

Lizard hesitates.

Then she unflashes her eyes and unflares her nostrils
and opens her lips back up.

"*Baonjour*," she says again.
"*Baonjour*," I reply.

Lizard's Mother

She could stand to lose fifty pounds.
I'm not the one who says that, she is.
I like how she looks, with her soft squishy stomach
and soft bulgy arms and big soft hugs.

She needs to get her roots touched up.
I'm not the one who says that, she is.
There is a gray stripe on both sides
of her crooked part, and the rest of her hair is black,
like Lizard's,
and Lizard's sister Sara,
but not like Lizard's sister Mojo,
whose hair is partly black and partly green and partly pink.

She is always a day late and a dollar short.
She's the one who says that, too.
A lot of things are old and broken at Lizard's house.
The couch cushions are sunk-in,
and one of them has a big brown stain on it.
"It's not poop!" Lizard's mother says
with a laugh. "It just looks like it!"
The toilet in the downstairs bathroom keeps running
unless you jiggle the handle just right.
The front porch light has been burned out
for as long as I've known Lizard.

But her mom thinks everything Lizard and I do is great,
not *too* great, like if she made a big huge *thing* about it.
Just the right amount of great.

So when I said we should keep our project a secret,
Lizard knew I didn't mean
keep it a secret from *her* mother,
but keep it secret from *mine*.

"What are you two up to now?" Lizard's mother asks,
when she hears us on Wednesday afternoon
practicing saying *A la pairshoyn*,
which means "good-bye" in Guernésiais.
Usually she's at work on weekdays,
but today she stayed home with a bad cough and a stuffy nose.
But even if she wasn't here,
our parents don't mind if we spend time together
at each other's houses while they are at work,
because we've been best friends so long.

Lizard's house is just three blocks from mine.
We don't walk to school together in the morning,
because Lizard's family is often late for things.
But we walk home together,
either to her house or to mine,
almost every day,
except for Fridays,
when I bike to my piano lesson at four o'clock.

It's like my house is Lizard's house,
and Lizard's house is my house.
Both houses are *our* houses.

"We're saving a language that's going extinct,"
Lizard explains to her mother now.

Her mom doesn't ask which language,
or why it's going extinct,
or how two sixth-grade kids can save it.

All she says is "Great!"
Then she settles into her big reclining armchair,
which is permanently stuck in recliner mode,
and clicks on the TV.

Lizard's Father

He's never there.
Well, hardly ever.
Weeks can go by when I don't see him,
and then I only get a glimpse of him,
on the way to the bathroom or something.
That's why Lizard says he's a spy.

You might think I'd roll my eyes and say,
"Nobody's father in Benson, Colorado, is a spy!
What does he really do?"

But I don't.

It has to be some job where he works at night
and sleeps during the day,
since her mom sometimes reminds Lizard to be quiet
because her dad is sleeping.
Except I can't think of any night job
Lizard wouldn't want people to know about.

I've never seen Lizard cry,
which seems strange, since she and I have been best friends
since third grade.
How could Lizard never cry
once during three whole years?

But it's true.

So I don't ever ask her about her father,
just in case that might be the first time
I'd see my best friend cry.

Our Clubhouse

No one has lived in the house next door
to Lizard's for a long time.
The windows are boarded up,
and the weeds grow wild like a meadow.

But the house next door is our favorite
because it has an old shed in back that isn't locked.
Lizard and I have it as our private clubhouse.

We even keep some furniture there:
a card table with one broken leg that we prop up,
and two chairs that were on someone's front lawn
with a sign that said FREE,
and a bunch of cushions with limp stuffing
that we use to make a nest
where we can curl up together.
I write poems,
and Lizard makes plans
for how the two of us can save the world.

On Thursday we go out there
to practice our Guernésiais.

Now we're really saving the world,
or at least a tiny part of it,

one word at a time.

What Lizard and I Figure Out

It's hard for two kids
to learn a language,
even a little bit of one,
all by themselves.

When I took that after-school French class,
Madame Jones would say something to us in French,
and we'd repeat it to her.
Then she'd tell us
whether we pronounced the words
right or wrong.

Even if Madame Jones's accent wasn't very good,
compared to the accent of a real French person from France,
it was probably ten thousand times better than our accents
when we try to speak Guernésiais.

Now we don't have any teacher at all.

On the internet Lizard and I found these little videos
called "Conversations in Guernésiais,"
where an old woman and an old man
sit at a table and talk about the weather,
or what they are going to eat for lunch,
or what they are going to plant in their garden.
While they talk, the words appear on the screen
in Guernésiais and in English.

Lizard and I keep pausing the videos so that we can try
to repeat the words that are supposed to mean
"It's raining hard" or "I grow potatoes."

But the old people on the video can't hear us,
to tell us if we said the words right or wrong.

If real Guernésiais people from the Isle of Guernsey heard us,
they'd think we were saying everything a thousand times worse
than the French teacher with the not-very-good accent.

But I hope they'd be grateful that two kids in America
were at least trying to save their language for them.

We Become the First Students in the History of Southern Peaks Middle School to Speak Guernésiais in the Cafeteria at Lunchtime

On Sunday afternoon,
after we spend half an hour
practicing how to say
"It's sunny today" and
"I'm planting carrots,"
Lizard says it's time we started
speaking Guernésiais at school.
Well, the little bit we know.

So the next day at our lunch table,
the one by the window where we always sit,
Lizard says, "Bumble, *comme tchi que l'affaire va?*"
which means "How are you?"
And I say,
"*En amas bian,*"
which means "Things are good."

Veronica, Zoey, and Zari look at one another.

Then Veronica says, "Huh?"

Two Hundred Plus Five

Lizard explains how thousands of languages
are going to be lost from the world forever.

Veronica, Zoey, and Zari are as amazed
as Lizard was when I first told her.

Lizard explains how she's going to save one of them.
She makes it sound like it was all her idea,
which I guess it was.

Lizard explains how she went on the internet
and picked Guernésiais as the language to save.
I guess that was all her idea, too.

"So," Lizard says,
when she's finished explaining everything,
and I haven't said anything,
"Bumble and I have been learning Guernésiais,
and now we're going to teach it to you."

She doesn't add "Okay?"
but that's okay,
because this time she said "Bumble and I,"
and this time she said "we."

By the time we have eaten our tacos
and Spanish rice and refried beans,
there are now three more people at Southern Peaks Middle School
who are speaking Guernésiais.

The number of people in the world who speak some Guernésiais is no longer two hundred plus two.

Now it's two hundred plus five.

Two Strange Things

When I get home that afternoon from Lizard's house,
after learning how to say *"Coume tchi qu't'as naom?"*
which means "What is your name?" in Guernésiais,
my mother is just getting home, too.
Some days I get home first,
some days she gets home first,
and some days my father gets home first.
But all of us always get home by six
to have dinner together.

Strange thing number one:
Even though it's Monday,
and the meetings she hates are on Mondays,
she doesn't say a single thing about George Bixler
and how *insufferable* he is,
and how he is trying to steer graduate students
away from working with her
because he claims that studying
almost-dead languages
is a completely dead end
for a career in linguistics.
She doesn't even mention him.

Strange thing number two:
Even though she knows that Mr. J
was going to return the math exams today,
and math is my worst subject,
and this test is worth 20 percent
of my trimester grade,
she doesn't ask me what I got on it.

She just says,
"I'm going upstairs for a while.
When your father gets home,
can you tell him
there's leftover beef bourguignon in the fridge
he can heat up for dinner?"

She's gone before I can say,
"Aren't you hungry?"
She's gone before I can say,
"I got an eighty-seven!"
She's gone before I can ask,
"Is everything okay?"

But I wouldn't have been brave enough
to ask that anyway.

Beef Bourguignon for Two

When I tell Dad
that Mom told me
that I should tell him
to heat up the beef bourguignon for dinner,
all he does is get the container of leftovers
out of the fridge.

He doesn't ask, "Is Mom okay?"

Somehow I know this means
he already knows she's not okay.

But not okay how?

So after he dumps yesterday's beef bourguignon,
which is a fancy kind of beef stew,
into my mother's favorite big, enameled,
deep-blue cast-iron Le Creuset pot,
which came all the way from France,
the country where they speak the language
that Guernésiais sort of sounds like,
I ask him,
"Is Mom okay?"

"She's under a lot of stress,"
he finally says.
"You know how challenging her work is.
It's just a lot for her right now.
Especially with waiting to hear about the grant.
And, well, you know how she is.
You know how she gets."

I do know exactly how she is.
I do know exactly how she gets.

But she's always under a lot of stress,
and this is the first time she's ever left us
to eat beef bourguignon from the recipe
in Julia Child's *Mastering the Art of French Cooking*
without her.

Afterward

We don't see my mom
for the rest of the evening.

But at breakfast the next morning,
she fixes me scrambled eggs
and buttered toast,
and pours me orange juice,
just like an ordinary morning.

She asks,
"Did you get your math test back?"

And this is the first time
I've ever been glad
to have my mother ask
about one of my math tests.

Guernésiais versus Spanish

At lunch on Tuesday, Veronica and Zoey
have already forgotten the words they learned yesterday.
Zari is the only one who remembers.

But after she says the Guernésiais
for "Hello, how are you?"
she says, "Wouldn't it be better for us to learn
a useful language, like Spanish?"

Lizard does her eye-flashing, nostril-flaring,
lip-pinching thing she usually only does with me.

"Spanish doesn't need saving!
Millions and millions of people speak Spanish!
Look at South America!
It's a whole continent filled
with people who speak Spanish!"

Well, people in Brazil speak Portuguese,
which I know because of my mother.
But I'm not about to point this out right now.

"There are people right here in the United States,"
Zari continues,
"right here in Colorado,
right here in our *school*,
who speak Spanish.
They speak English, too,
but don't you want to be able to talk to them
in the language they love best?"

It's true that the Spanish-speaking kids
at our school sit together at lunch
and speak Spanish to one another the whole time.

Lizard hesitates.
Zari is the best at sounding calm and reasonable
of any kid I know.

Then Lizard says,
"We can learn more than one language, you know.
We can learn Guernésiais *and* Spanish."

"In Europe everybody knows tons of languages,"
I add to be helpful.

"This isn't Europe," Veronica says quickly.
I know this means she doesn't want to learn
either language, let alone both.

Then Zoey says,
"I heard that the fall musical
is going to be *Alice in Wonderland*."

"I love *Alice in Wonderland*!"
Veronica says.
"I've seen the Disney movie
fifteen times."

Zari says,
"I heard that the auditions for it are next week.
"But if you want to audition,
you have to sign up by Friday."

And that is the end of today's
lunchtime Guernésiais lesson.

Alice in Lunch Table Land

At lunch on Wednesday
everyone at our table
(except Lizard and me)
has a reason
why she should be Alice.
Zoey went to tap-dancing camp last summer.
"Does Alice tap-dance?" Lizard asks.
"I bet she doesn't."

Veronica has watched the Disney movie of Alice
fifteen times,
which she has now already told us
fifteen times.
"Just because you've *watched* a musical,
doesn't mean you'd be good
at being *in* a musical," Lizard says.
"Besides, Mr. Delgado isn't doing
the Disney version with the Disney songs.
He has some other version of his own."

Zari has a great big beautiful voice.
Actually, she doesn't say that about herself.
So I say it:
"Zari has a great big beautiful voice."

"But Zari doesn't look like Alice," Veronica says.
"Alice has blond hair, and—well . . ."
She doesn't finish the sentence,
but I know she means, "Zari is Black."

"Who says Alice has blond hair?" Lizard demands.

"She just does," Veronica says. "She's blond in the movie."

"She's not blond in my head," Lizard says.
"In my head Alice could totally look like Zari."

Zari gives Lizard a small smile.

Sometimes I'm extra glad I'm best friends with Lizard.

But Sometimes I'm Not

"You know who looks like Alice?" Zoey says.

When nobody answers, she points at me.

"Bumble?!" Lizard says.

She makes it sound like, in her head,
I'm the only person in the world
who could never be Alice.

"Her hair is blond," Zoey says. "Well, dishwater blond.
She's even wearing a black headband."

"Anybody can wear a black headband!" Lizard says.
"Millions of people wear black headbands!"

Zoey doesn't give up.
"Plus, Betsy has, I don't know, a wondering kind of face."

I never thought of anybody else thinking
about what kind of face I have.
It makes me feel like I'm real, like I *exist*,
not just in my own head but in the world.

"Anyway," Lizard says, "Bumble can't sing.
Zari should be Alice."

I agree.
Zari should be Alice.

But part of me wants to say to Lizard,
"Maybe I can sing,
and you just never listened.
Maybe I do have a wondering kind of face,
and you just never noticed."

What I Start Wondering Now

I was in a play once,
last year in fifth grade,
because everyone in the class was in it.

It was a play about immigrants coming to Ellis Island.
I was a girl from Poland.
I wore a flowered kerchief over my head
and clutched an old-fashioned suitcase
one of the class parents had donated as a prop.

On the night of the play,
the lights were so bright when it was my turn to come onstage
that I felt terrified and lost and confused, but excited, too,
just like a Polish girl named Zofia would have felt,
waiting in a long line of immigrants
to see if she would be welcomed into her new country.

After I said my lines
the audience clapped for me,
and for Zofia, and for me being Zofia.

So when Zoey said what she said about me at lunch,
I started wondering if
maybe . . . maybe . . .
it would be fun to be in a play again,
this time wearing,
not a flowered kerchief,
but maybe . . . maybe . . .
a black headband?

Amazing

It's amazing how just one thing
said by just one person,
in the middle of just one conversation
on just one regular day,

can start a person wondering things

she had never wondered

before.

Signing Up

"You're kidding," Lizard says,
when I'm five minutes late on Friday
to meet her at her locker after school
because I was signing up on the audition sheet
on Mr. Delgado's door.

"I think it would be fun to be in a play,"
I say, keeping my voice light and cheerful.

"You and everyone else,"
Lizard says,
as if it's a bad thing to want to do anything
lots of other people want to do.

"I probably won't even get picked to be in it,"
I say.

I don't know if I'm trying to reassure Lizard
that she doesn't have to worry I might actually
do something without her,
something she didn't decide for us both to do,
or if I'm trying to prepare myself
not to be disappointed
if I really don't get picked.

Either way, Lizard's face brightens.

How to Make My Mother Very, Very Happy

Tell her that you're auditioning for *Alice in Wonderland*.

When she asks if this was Lizard's idea,
tell her no, it was your own idea.

Add that Lizard didn't even sign up on the audition sheet.

Smile when she says,
"Oh, Betsy, you'd be perfect as Alice!"

Keep smiling when she says,
"Maybe *this* will be the year you start to bloom!"
(unlike third grade, fourth grade, and fifth grade,
when your lack of blooming
was somehow Lizard's fault).

Don't stop smiling even when she says,
"When are the auditions?
Maybe we can get you a couple
of voice lessons first."

Just remember how good it feels
to see your mother smiling,

and to know she's smiling
because of you.

But the Smile Doesn't Last

The very next day
my mother makes Moroccan chicken for dinner,
after a long day working in her office upstairs.
(She works on Saturdays and Sundays, too,
because dying languages don't stop dying
on weekends.)

But just like last week with the beef bourguignon,
she doesn't eat the Moroccan chicken
with my father and me.

And on Sunday,
she doesn't eat the asparagus risotto with us,
either.

Moroccan chicken and asparagus risotto
don't taste as good
when the person who made them
is upstairs in her bedroom
with the door closed.

Auditioning for a Play Is Much Scarier Than Shots, Dogs That Bite, or Worms on a Rainy Day

It's scary having to tell Lizard
not to wait for me after school on Tuesday,
because that's when I have my audition,
and seeing her toss her head
as if she never planned on waiting for me
anyway.

It's scary sitting in the auditorium
waiting for my turn to get up on the big, bare stage
as half the girls at Southern Peaks Middle School
show how they can sing
ten thousand times better than me.

It's even scarier hearing Mr. Delgado call my name,
and walking up onto the big, bare stage by myself,
and making myself open my mouth,
and hearing my squeaky little voice
in that big, empty space,
then walking down the three steps from the stage
and being so worried about tripping
that somehow I trip and bang my knee anyway.

It's scariest of all coming home
and having my mother ask me,
"How did the audition go?"

Then having to tell her,
"Not so good."

Then having her say, hopefully,
"I bet it went better than you think."

Then making myself say, "Maybe,"
so she can go on hoping

a little bit longer.

What If?

What if my mother is right
and the audition did go better than I thought?

What if I get a part, but it's not Alice,
when my mother is so hoping I'll be Alice?

What if I was terrible at the audition
and I don't get any part at all,
and Lizard says, "See?"

What if I get a great part
and my mother is thrilled
but Lizard is furious?

What if I get an awful part
and Lizard is happy
but my mother is heartbroken?

What if there isn't any "what if"
that doesn't make at least one person
end up being miserable?

What if the person who ends up
most miserable of all
is me?

Imaginary Grandparents

Between practicing the audition song
(which sounded so pitiful and pathetic
when I sang it yesterday)
and dreading the audition results
(which are going to be posted on Friday),
I almost forget I'm supposed to be
practicing Guernésiais with Lizard.

But Lizard doesn't forget.

On Wednesday we're at her house,
and the old woman and the old man
are talking about going to the beach.

"Do you think they're married in real life?"
I ask. "Or are they just old friends?
Maybe her husband died,
and his wife died, so now
they spend their lonely days
just sitting and conversing together."

"I think they're married," Lizard says.
"And the trip to the beach
is with their grandkids."

"Yes! I wish they were *our* grandparents!"
My grandparents, and Lizard's, too,
live far away and we hardly ever see them.

So the next day,
when it's Guernésiais time,
I say, "Let's go visit Grandma and Grandpa."

Lizard laughs, but then she says,
"Hey, maybe we could go on a trip sometime
to the Isle of Guernsey and meet them!
Like if we get invited there to get a prize
for all we've done to help save their language."

This is the unlikeliest idea yet
of Lizard's unlikely ideas.

But it's a happy idea in a not-so-happy week,
with me worried about the audition results
and my mom worried about getting her big grant
and even my dad looking worried,
because he worries when we worry.

So I grin at Lizard and say,
"Maybe we could!"

Audition Results

Mr. Delgado said he'd post them
on his office door
when the closing buzzer sounds
at 3:12 p.m. on Friday.

Will it jinx things if I race there
the instant the bell rings?
Maybe it's bad luck to let the universe
see how much you want something.
Would it be better to stroll toward his door
casually, as if I'm heading somewhere else,
and then act like I suddenly remembered:
"Oh, that's right, weren't the audition results
going to be posted today?"

Then Lizard is right there beside me.

"Someone we don't know is Alice,"
Lizard says.
"Zari is the Queen of Hearts.
You and Zoey and Veronica are flowers.

Some of the flowers have names
and get to say lines.
Veronica is Lily.
The extra flowers
don't have names or speak lines.
You and Zoey are extra flowers."

I can't tell if she's glad
because she knew the audition results first,
the way she always knows everything first,
or if she's glad because she was right
that the last person in the world
who would ever have been picked
to be Alice

is me.

Extra Flowers

I follow Lizard to the throng of kids
in front of Mr. Delgado's office door.

Veronica is actually crying about being a flower,
even though she's the only one of us
whose flower has a name.

"I've wanted to be Alice my whole entire life!"
she wails. "I've seen the movie fifteen times,
and every single time I thought
that would be *me* someday."

Zoey doesn't seem to mind being an extra flower.
"At least we're both extra flowers," she tells me.

We can't even get close to Zari
because so many people are hugging her.
The Queen of Hearts is the next-best part
after Alice.

"You're not going to *be* an extra flower, are you?"
Lizard asks me, in a low voice.

I don't understand the question.

"That's the part Mr. Delgado gave me.
That's the part I have to be."

"No you don't," Lizard says.
She sounds almost angry.
At Mr. Delgado? At me?
"You don't have to be in the play at all."

Now I understand.

Why would I spend hours at boring rehearsals
to be one of five extra flowers,
when instead I could spend those same hours
with our imaginary grandparents,
helping to save Guernésiais with her?

Telling My Mother

"I'm an extra flower,"
I blurt out the instant
she walks through the front door
so she won't bother asking.

"Oh," she says.

She quickly forces a smile.

"But I'm so proud of you for trying!
A little part this time
can lead to a bigger part next time!"

I can see from the crease in her forehead
that now she's pretty sure
this isn't going to be the year
I start blooming, either.

Through, technically, extra flowers
are blooming,
just not in my mother's sense
of *blooming*.

Then I blurt out what parts
everybody else got
so she won't have to ask,
"Did any of your friends
get real parts?"

Though, technically, any part
is a real part,
just not in my mother's sense
of *real*.

"I'm so proud of you for trying,"
she says again, and gives me a hug this time.

I think she said it twice
because she was afraid I wouldn't believe her
if she only said it once.

Or maybe she said it twice
because she needs to work twice as hard
to believe it herself.

Telling My Father

"Wow!" he says at dinner,
when the three of us are eating
Chinese food he picked up on the way home
from the woodworking studio space
he rents on the other side of town.
"My daughter, the flower!"

I don't remind him
that I'm only an extra flower.

"Does Mr. Delgado need any parents
to help with building the set?
Tell him your dad is the best there is
with a saw and a hammer."

"I will!"

My dad is also the best there is
at making someone believe
that being an extra flower
is perfectly fine.

No, perfectly wonderful.

My First Fight with Lizard

"You're really going to be an extra flower,
hanging around in the auditorium forever
watching other people be Alice
and the Queen of Hearts
and the Caterpillar
and the Mad Hatter
and Tweedle Dum and Tweedle Dee
and flowers that have actual *names*?"

We are at Lizard's on Saturday morning
in our nest in the clubhouse,
but instead of thumbing through the latest
"Learn Guernésiais" booklet she found online
and printed out on her mom's printer,
she's still arguing with me about the play.

I hate arguing with anybody about anything.
But even more I hate arguing
with Lizard about this.
I think this might be the first fight
we've ever had,
maybe because every other time
I let her win before we even started fighting.

But I'm not giving in this time.

"Yes!
Now can we please talk about something else?"

Will Lizard be so angry
she'll never speak to me again?
Will Lizard be so furious
that we won't be best friends anymore?

But all she says is
"Okay. If that's what you want."

Something in the way her lips tremble
make me think this just missed
being my first time
to see Lizard cry.

The Alice Flowers

I had a conversation once with Lizard
about whether animals have souls.
We decided they did,
because we didn't want to go to heaven
if dogs and cats couldn't go there, too
(even though neither of us have a dog or cat
because our parents won't let us).

Then Lizard asked if plants have souls,
and we decided maybe not all plants,
like maybe not broccoli or lima beans,
but probably flowers have small fragrant souls
because in heaven beautiful flowers
would be blooming everywhere.

So I was surprised to find out,
at our first rehearsal on Tuesday,
that the flowers in *Alice in Wonderland*
are *not* flowers who are going to end up
in any heaven *I'd* want to go to.

They are snobby, snooty, *mean* flowers
who make fun of Alice
because her petals aren't curly enough
(they think she's a flower, too,
only one with a strange shape),
and they call her names like stupid
because she doesn't understand
anything about Wonderland yet
and she doesn't fit in anywhere.

I don't know how I feel now
about being an extra *mean* flower.

But maybe the extra flowers in Wonderland
don't have as much reason to be snobby and snooty,
and so aren't as mean
as the flowers that have actual names
and get to speak actual lines.

More about Mean Flowers

The mean flowers in the play
are clearly supposed to be like
the cool, popular girls
in books about middle school,
who sit at the cool, popular lunch table,
where the less-cool, less-popular girls
are dying to sit but can't,
because they aren't sufficiently
cool or popular,
at least in the eyes of the
reigning cool, popular girls.

But at Southern Peaks Middle School,
we don't have a lunch table like that,
or if we do, I am so uncool and so unpopular
that I don't even know which one it is.

Lizard and I wouldn't want
to sit there anyway.

The Language of Flowers

Mr. Delgado says
all of the extra flowers
are going to be roses.
I'm going to be a yellow rose.
Zoey is going to be a pink rose.

When I tell my parents at dinner that night
(relieved that my mother is at dinner that night)
that their daughter is now a yellow rose,
my mother gets a dreamy look on her face.

"When I was in high school
my friend Alison read somewhere
that if a boy gave you a rose,
the color of the rose meant something special.
A red rose meant he loved you passionately.
A pink rose meant he loved you, but not as much.
A yellow rose meant he just wanted to be friends.
Yellow was supposed to be the color of friendship,
at least when it came to roses.

So when my high school boyfriend gave me
yellow roses for my birthday, I burst out crying,
to his great bewilderment and disappointment.

But it turned out none of the boys
had ever heard of how the color of roses
was, according to Alison, supposed to be
the secret language of love."

Nothing to Worry About

The flowers, including the extra flowers,
only have their rehearsals
after school on Tuesday and Thursday.

So I'm *not* going to be spending endless hours
watching other people practice their real parts,
wasting precious time I could have spent
helping the people on the Isle of Guernsey
save their dying language.

Besides
(though I can't say this to Lizard
or to my mother),
it's going to be fun being an extra flower.

We sing the same song
as the flowers-with-names.

We do the same dance,
all of the flowers together.

I'm going to have flower makeup
and wear a flower costume.

I can take off two afternoons a week
from saving Guernésiais, right?

I can take off two afternoons a week
from being Lizard's friend, right?

I Turn Out to Be a Genius

"What are we going to do about
Zari, Veronica, and Zoey?"
Lizard asks me on Wednesday afternoon,
as we watch cartoons on Lizard's TV
and eat an entire bag of Ruffles potato chips
with sour-cream-and-onion dip.
(Even Lizard needs a break
from language practice sometimes.)

"What are we going to do about them
about *what*?" I ask.

"About you-know-what," Lizard says.

"If I *knew* what, I wouldn't *ask* what."

"About Guernésiais, dummy!
They couldn't care less about it.
All they care about is the play,
the play, the stupid play!"
She glares at me because she knows
I care a lot about the play these days, too,
even though I've just been
to one rehearsal so far.

I try to think of something helpful
to say, but it's hard.

"I don't know.
Maybe we need to find some *other* people
to save it with us, people who would actually
want to save it, too."

"Like who?" Lizard demands.
The two of us don't exactly have
a million friends.

"Maybe we could start a club,
a Guernésiais-saving club,
and advertise it with posters in the halls
and a morning announcement,
so lots of kids would know about it and join."

Then Lizard says something
I've never heard her say before:
"Bumble. You. Are. A. Genius."

What It Takes to Make a Club

"You have to have a faculty adviser,"
Lizard says.

I have no idea how she knows this
since she's the one who said when school started
that we shouldn't be in any clubs
because clubs are dumb.

"When my sister Sara made her origami club,
she found a teacher to sponsor it.
When my sister Mojo wanted to make an Anti-Club Club
for all the kids who hate clubs,
she had to find a faculty sponsor, too."

"Did she?" I ask. "Find one?"

"Of course not!"

"So who can *we* find
for our club?"

Lizard's face lights up.
"The French teacher!
Ms.—what's her name—Fletcher.
Because you said Guernésiais is sort of like French."

At Southern Peaks you can start taking
foreign languages in seventh grade,
which my mother says is ridiculous,
because why leave out the sixth graders?
The younger you are, she says,
the *better* you are at learning languages
because of something that has to do with your brain.

Maybe Lizard and I should have tried to save
Guernésiais back in elementary school,
but of course Lizard didn't know about
the lost languages then.

But if we start a Guernésiais-saving club,
lots and lots of kids will know about
the lost languages now.

Guess Who Walks into Lizard's Living Room?

Lizard's father!

"Hey, Bumble," he says,
as if he just saw me yesterday.
"How're things these days with Bumbleweed?"

I'm surprised he remembers that joke he used
to make years ago
about Lizard's name for me.
Apparently, there's some old song
about "tumbling tumbleweeds,"
and he liked singing it to me,
only changing it to "tumbling bumbleweeds."

"They're okay," I say.

"School okay?" he asks then,
and I nod.

I'm not going to ask him,
"How're things these days with you, Mr. Angelino?
Spying okay?"

His hair is uncombed,
and his cheeks and chin are grizzly,
but my father looks like that, too,
when he's in the middle of a huge job.

Mr. Angelino's eyes are red,
what my mom calls "bloodshot,"
which doesn't sound like
a good thing for eyes to be.

He whistles the tumbling bumbleweed song
cheerfully as he heads past us to the kitchen,
and Lizard goes back to talking about our club
as if we were never interrupted.

But as he whistles,
I get a whiff of his breath,
and it smells like the half-empty glasses
all over the living room
after my parents have their dreaded once-a-year party
for the people in the linguistics department.

And now I think I know
what Lizard's father does
instead of spying.

The Most Stuck-Up Flower of All

Just last week
Veronica was crying
in front of everybody
because she had to be a flower
instead of being Alice.

Now, at lunch on Thursday,
she acts as if the title of the play
were *Lily in Wonderland.*

I know that the flowers in the play are
supposed to be stuck-up and think they are
so beautiful and so wonderful,
but in my opinion
the actor-flowers in real life
don't have a lot to brag about,
names or no names,
especially if your flower only has
one line
that you speak all by yourself.

There is no reason for Veronica
to complain that she couldn't finish her math homework
because she was too busy practicing her lines
and singing the flower song
to herself in the mirror.

There is no reason for Veronica
to tell Zoey and me that we shouldn't be sad
because in the musical next year
we both might get real parts, too.

At Our Second Rehearsal

Zoey and I sit together in the back
of the auditorium waiting
for the flowers to have their turn.

Veronica—I mean Lily—is sitting
up front with Rose, Larkspur, Violet, and Daisy.

"I wish *I* was the flower who gets to say,
'We *can* talk when there is anybody
worth talking to,'" Zoey says.
"Then *I'd* be worthy of sitting
with the *fancy* flowers, too."

We both crack up,
and then we're laughing so hard
we can hardly breathe,
gasping to get the giggles out.

I never noticed before that Zoey is funny.

I wonder what other things
I never noticed about her, too.

Things I'm Noticing Now about Zoey

She likes to read.
She has a big long book with her.
"In case I get bored," she says.
She tells me about it, and it sounds wonderful.
"You can borrow it when I'm done," she offers.
"I think it's your kind of book."

When she goes to the food table to get snacks,
she brings back two chocolate chip cookies for her
and two oatmeal raisin cookies for me.
"I know you like oatmeal raisin," she says,
and it's true, but I can't remember
ever telling her that.

All along Zoey has been noticing more things
about me

than I ever noticed
about her.

A Club Is Born

"I don't know, girls," Ms. Fletcher says,
when we find her in the French classroom
after school on Friday
before I have to head home
to get ready for my piano lesson.

"There are so many clubs at Southern Peaks already,
from Chess Club to Manga Club, and a dozen more.
I can't see the need for another one.
I'm already advising the French Club,
and I don't know of any other Southern Peaks teacher
who has taken on *two* after-school obligations."

Lizard's eyes flash.
Lizard's nostrils flare.

"Languages are *going extinct*.
Languages are going to be lost *forever*.
Thousands of them!
You're a *language* teacher!
Can't you give one hour a week
to help us save at least *one*?"

So what can Ms. Fletcher do but sigh and say,
"All right, I'll fill out the necessary paperwork.
But, girls, I don't think . . ."

She doesn't finish the sentence.
So we never get to find out what our new club adviser
doesn't think about our new club.

Posters!

We make the posters on Saturday afternoon
at my house,
because my mom has a color printer,
and the printer at Lizard's house
is only black-and-white.

The posters say:

SAVE GUERNÉSIAIS!

Did you know that hundreds of languages in the world are DYING?

Do you want to help a dying language LIVE?

Only 205 people in the world speak Guernésiais.

You can be #206!

Then we put the when-and-where information
for our organizational club meeting,
which will take place after school on Wednesday
in Ms. Fletcher's French classroom.

On some posters we put the flag of Guernsey
(a yellow cross on a red cross on a white background).
On some we put a photo of the coast of Guernsey
with a beckoning path.
On some we put a photo of a Guernsey village
with tall houses clustered together by the sea.

"Maybe one of those houses
belongs to our grandparents,"
I say.

"I wish they knew about us,"
Lizard says.
"I wish they knew we were making a club
for them."

And I say,
"I do, too."

Saving the Surprise

My mom is supposed to be at the university,
meeting one of her graduate students at three o'clock.
(Yes, she meets with students on weekends.)

So Lizard and I are startled when we hear her voice,
complaining to my father that the student didn't show up.

"Quick! Hide the posters!"
I shout-whisper to Lizard.

My mom comes into her office
just as Lizard is snatching the last poster
from the printer.

"We're printing something for a school project,"
I explain quickly.

"What school project?" my mom asks.
(She loves school projects.)

"It's for social studies."

Too late, I remember that Lizard and I
aren't in the same social studies class,
and this is the kind of thing
my mom would remember.

"It's for Lizard's class," I add.
"Because it has to be in color,
and Lizard doesn't have
the right kind of printer."

I hope my mom doesn't notice
that a stack of fifty posters
is awfully thick for a school project.

"You're welcome to use our printer
anytime, Lizard," my mom says.
"Good luck with your project!"

Lizard bursts out laughing
when we're back in my room.

"Wait till she finds out that
we're really helping *her* with *her* project!"
Lizard says, hugging herself with happiness.
"Just wait till she finds out!"

Saturday Night Bombshell

Dinner tonight is pesto pasta with artichokes.
Even though we don't usually have dessert,
tonight we have three different flavors of gelato
that my father bought for a special treat.

"We have some news to share,"
my mother says
after I take the first bite of hazelnut gelato,
which is my favorite flavor.

I have a terrible feeling it's bad news.
My mother is smiling,
but I can't tell if it's a fake smile
or a real smile.

When Eloise's parents got divorced,
Lizard told me Eloise had no idea
they weren't madly in love
until the day they told her that her dad
was leaving to marry someone else.

But my father would never leave
my mother and me.

And my mother is too busy with her work
to fall in love with anybody new.

"What is it?" I ask,
glad that gelato is a food
that slips down your throat
even if your throat
has a huge terrified lump in it.

My mother gives another
maybe-real, maybe-fake smile.

"Your father,"
she says,
"is going on a trip."

Dad's Trip

An important architect asked Dad
to make the furniture
for an important house he's building
for an important client,
who lives somewhere in North Carolina,
so he's paying for Dad to fly there
to meet the client,
and see the halfway-finished house,
and how it fits into the setting,
and study exactly how the Smoky Mountains look
at sunrise and probably at sunset, too,
for inspiration.

(Plus, Dad can visit my great-aunt,
who lives in a nearby town,
all alone in a falling-down house,
and who could use a visit from
somebody handy with tools to check up on things.)

It does sound like the coolest trip ever,
and my dad has the coolest job ever,
and I'm the proudest daughter ever.

But

"How long you will be gone?" I ask him,
and I can't keep the wobble out of my voice.

"Two weeks," he says.

Two weeks without Dad making Belgian waffles
for my mom and me on Sunday mornings
and bringing them to us in my parents' bed.

Two weeks without Dad running the vacuum
in between times when the every-other-week cleaner comes
because Mom gets extra stressed if the house is extra dirty.

Two weeks without Dad putting his arms around Mom
and telling her that George Bixler is bound
to retire one of these days
and she shouldn't let *him* take up space in *her* head.

Two weeks without Dad winking at me
if Mom gets on my case about practicing piano.

Two weeks without Dad smiling at me every morning
and saying, "Good morning, Sunshine."

Two weeks without Dad tucking me into bed every night
even though I'm almost twelve.

Two weeks!

Questions

"When are you leaving?" I ask him.

"Actually, soon," he says.

"How soon?"

"Actually, tomorrow," he says.

"Tomorrow?!"

"I know," he says.

"They've been pressuring me to go,
and I kept dithering and dithering.
I just didn't know how you and your mother . . .
After all, she works so hard,
she's so crazy busy,
and has so much going on,
and I like to be here to help
with whatever I can.

And two weeks—
well, two weeks—

it's just a long time."

"Now, James"

My mother lays her hand on his arm
and shakes her head
as if to put a stop to his foolishness.

"You know how much I want you
to have this opportunity!
Betsy wants you to have it, too.

Heaven knows it's your turn.
Every high-end cabinetmaker in America
would leap at this chance.

And poor Aunt Etta needs you right now
more than we do. You've been worried
about her for ages!

James, we will be fine!
Betsy, tell him:
You and I will be totally fine!"

So I Tell Him

"Daddy, Mom and I
will be fine!
Truly we will."

But even as I say this
with a great big smile,
I can't help thinking:

A month without my mom
isn't all that long
for my dad and me.

Two weeks without my dad
will be an eternity
for my mom and me.

On the Way to the Airport on Sunday Morning

Nobody talks very much,
except for my dad.

"Betsy, at least I'll be back in plenty of time
to see my flower in the play."

"Kathleen, don't let those clowns get you down."
Only he says a different word for *clowns*.

"I sure hope I can find a way to help Aunt Etta
stay in that wreck of a house."

"I'll call every night, okay?"

"I'll be back before you know it."

"Well, I guess we're here."

Mom pulls up to the curb
where all the other cars are pulling up
to drop off all the other people.

Mom and I get out of the car to hug him,
and I know that none of those other people
are going to miss their other people
as much as we're going to miss him.

The First Night without Dad

It's okay.

My mother lights candles for dinner
the way she always does, even though
now there are only two of us.

She asks me how the play is going.

"Fine," I say.

"Maybe you'll meet some new friends there,"
she says hopefully.

I don't tell her that I already have.
Well, just one, and not technically a *new* friend,
because Zoey and I were already friends,
but not the way we are getting to be now.

If I said that, it would make me
feel sad for Lizard.

"Maybe," I echo instead.

I clear the table and load the dishwasher.
She puts the leftover quiche and salad away.

I practice a Chopin nocturne
while she grades linguistics exams.
"Betsy, that sounds beautiful!"
she tells me when I'm done.
Nocturnes are sad, lonely music,
but somehow they make a sad, lonely evening
a little bit less sad and lonely
because the music knows how to say
what my mother and I
are both feeling inside.

When Dad's special ringtone
sounds on her cell phone,
we both run to the table to get it,
and even pretend to push and shove
to be the one to get it first.

And when I win the phone grab
and hear Dad's voice,
everything is even better than okay.

Snacks for the Club

"What kind of food do people eat in Guernsey?"
Lizard asks, when we're at her house
after school on Monday.

We got there later than usual today
because we spent half an hour
with two rolls of masking tape
putting up fifty SAVE GUERNÉSIAIS! posters
on every surface at Southern Peaks Middle School
where kids can put up posters.

"I don't know. Why?"

"We need snacks for the first club meeting,
and now it's just two days away.
If it's a club for saving the Guernsey language,
we should be serving Guernsey snacks,
don't you think?"

"Well, since Guernésiais is sort of like French,
maybe Guernsey snacks are sort of like French snacks?"

On the computer we look for more
information about Guernsey,
since we just looked for beautiful photos last time.
We learn that the people there
who don't speak Guernésiais
speak English, not French.

"So, maybe English food?" I suggest.
"Like English muffins?"

"People who come to a club to save Guernésiais
don't want to eat English muffins!"

Lizard is almost certainly right about that.

We find out that Guernsey is most famous for its . . . cows!

"We could have cheese," I say.

"Ooh!" Lizard licks her lips.
"Like that yummy cheese that comes
in those little foil triangles.
Laughing Cow!"

The name Laughing Cow
makes both of us laugh.

"We can borrow some of my mom's cow things,"
Lizard continues.

Lizard's mom collects anything with a cow on it:
cow potholders,
and cow dishtowels,
and cow tablecloths,
and cow salt-and-pepper shakers,
and cow mugs,
and little cheese spreaders
with cows on the handles.

Our club is going to have
the best snacks and best decorations
of any club at Southern Peaks,

plus helping to save a dying language,
which is more than the
Chess Club
or Manga Club
can say.

More Things I Learn about Zoey

At Tuesday's rehearsal
I find out she's an only child, like me.

"My parents wanted more kids," Zoey says.
"Like lots and lots of kids.
But that didn't work out
and all they ended up with was me.
Sometimes it feels—you know?—
like a lot of pressure,
to be *me*,
but also like I have to make it up to them
for the other kids
they didn't get to have."

It occurs to me that I don't know
why I never had any sisters or brothers.
I guess it's because even one kid
is a lot for someone who is trying to study
as many dying languages as my mother.
Maybe things would be easier for my mom
if she had no kids at all.

But I don't say this to Zoey.
I don't even want to say it to myself.

Then Zoey tells me she hates scary movies,
and I say, "I hate scary movies, too!"

Then I tell Zoey that I'm afraid of worms,
and she says she loves worms,
and even had a pet worm once
named Wormy Squirmy,
until one day he squirmed away.

Then we're laughing so hard
that we don't even hear Mr. Delgado
call out, "Flowers! Up on stage!"
And he has to say it again:
"Flowers! Calling all flowers!"

The Queen of Hearts

Zoey and I may talk and talk
whenever the flowers aren't rehearsing,
but we always stop talking when
the Queen of Hearts starts to sing.

At our lunch table, Zari is the quietest one.
(Zoey and I are pretty quiet, too.
Veronica usually does most of the talking,
and Lizard does the second most,
because after Veronica says something,
Lizard has to tell her why she's wrong about it.)

But in the play, the Queen of Hearts is not quiet.
She bosses everyone around all the time,
and if they don't do exactly
what they are supposed to do,
she shouts, "Off with their heads!"

Even though I'm doing an okay job as a mean flower,
I don't think I'm ever mean in real life.
Even though Zari is doing a fabulous job as the queen,
I don't think she would ever boss people around
in real life, either.

But then she shrieks, "Off with their heads!"
and does such an amazing job
that I wonder if in real life
she might secretly want to cut off
just a few people's heads
just a little tiny bit.

Morning Announcements

Ms. Fletcher arranged for there to be
a mention of that afternoon's club meeting
in the morning announcements on Wednesday.

After announcements about the boys' soccer game
and the girls' volleyball game,
the principal starts to read the thing
Lizard and I wrote out for him to say.
It's pretty much the same thing we wrote
on the fifty full-color posters
hanging on all the school walls.

But we had forgotten to write out
how to pronounce Guernésiais,
because that wasn't something we needed
to put on the posters.

So Mr. Norcross reads:
"Come to the first meeting of the Save—
of the Save—
GWER—Is it GWER? Or GERR?
I think its GWER—
of the Save GWER-NESS-EE-ACE Club
this afternoon in Room 203!"

Then he reads the part
about how it's a dying language,
and everybody should come to help save it.

He finishes by saying,
"I guess I'd better come to the meeting
so I can learn how to pronounce its name!
Ha-ha! Ha-ha!"

Mr. Norcross thinks he's very funny.
But he's not.

Still, when the principal makes an announcement
about your club over the PA system
for the whole school to hear,
it sounds like a real club
that's really going to happen,
for a real language
(with a hard-to-pronounce name)
that's really going to be saved.

What We Have at the First Meeting of the Save Guernésiais Club

Grape juice.

Laughing Cow cheese.

Ritz crackers to spread the cheese on.

Cheese spreaders with cows on the handles.

A cow tablecloth on the table.

Paper plates and paper cups with cows on them.
(Lizard's mom had some.)

Paper napkins with cows on them.
(Lizard's mom had some of those, too.)

Two cofounders of the club: Lizard and me.

One club adviser who didn't want to advise the club anyway . . .

and

nobody else.

What Ms. Fletcher Says

I'm sorry, girls.
I had a feeling that . . .
In any case . . .

Well, I applaud
you two
for trying.

Taking Down Fifty Posters

Ms. Fletcher tells us that it's our job
to take down the posters.

So we do.

I thought Lizard would rip them off the walls
and crumple them up
and hurl them into the recycling bins.

But she doesn't.

She just says,
"*This* is why languages die, Bumble!

This is why your mom
is so exhausted and stressed all the time!

This is why your mom needs us
more than ever!"

The Queen of Pies

At rehearsal on Thursday,
Zoey asks me, "Do you like pie?"

I assume this is another question
like the ones we talked about on Tuesday:
Do you have any brothers or sisters?
What kind of movies do you like?

"Of course!" I say.
"Who doesn't like pie?"

"I *love* pie," Zoey says.
"All kinds of pie.
I love eating pie.
But most of all,
I love baking pie.
My parents call me
the Queen of Pies."

There is something
about the way Zoey says this
that makes it sound different
from telling me that she once
had a pet named Wormy Squirmy.

"So I was wondering,"
Zoey continues,
"do you want to come over sometime?
Like maybe tomorrow afternoon?
And bake a pie with me?"

Now I get it.

"Um—sure!" I say.

Tomorrow is Friday,
when I usually have my piano lesson,
but this week my teacher is off
giving a concert in New York somewhere.

So what possible reason could I have
for saying no?

Reasons Why I Now Wish I Hadn't Said I'd Bake a Pie with Zoey

Reason number one: my mother.
I just can't face how happy she'll be
that I'm doing something
with somebody who isn't Lizard.

Reason number two: Lizard.
I just can't face how mad she'll be
that I'm doing something
with somebody who isn't her.

Sharing the News with My Mother

"Can I go to Zoey's house after school tomorrow?"
I ask my mother as soon as she comes through
the door from the garage into the kitchen.
"Zoey's mom will pick us up from school
and drive me home afterward."

I don't know if I'm making it sound like more of a big deal
by asking her right away,
or if I'd be making it sound like more of a big deal
if I asked her later,
as if it were a big wonderful announcement
I had to save until she was settled in
for the evening.

From the way her eyes light up
I already know she's going to say yes.

"Is Lizard going, too?"
my mother asks,
and I can tell what she hopes the answer will be.

"No. Just me,
because Zoey and I are in the play together."

"Of course," my mother says,
with a huge smile.
It's been weeks since I've seen her
smile like that.

So I guess I forgive her for being so thrilled
that her daughter is finally hanging out
with a friend who isn't Lizard.

How to Break the News to Lizard

Tell her first thing Friday morning
when you meet her by her locker.

But I don't.

Tell her during
science or math.

But I don't.

Tell her at lunch before the others
come sit down at our table.

But I don't.

Tell her when you are walking together
to PE after lunch.

But I don't.

Race up to her one minute before you're supposed
to meet Zoey and blurt out:

"Lizard-I'm-not-going-to-my-piano-lesson-today-
because-my-teacher-is-away-and-
Zoey-asked-me-if-I'd-come-to-her-house-
to-bake-a-pie-and-so-I'm-going-there-okay?"

This time Lizard doesn't do
the flashing eyes and the flaring nostrils.
She just shrugs her shoulders
and holds her hands out, palms up,
as if to say, "Why would you think I'd even care?"

But I know she does.

Baking a Pie with Zoey

Zoey's mother leaves us alone in the kitchen,
because Zoey knows everything there is to know
about baking pies.
She is the *Empress* of Pies.

(An empress is even grander than a queen
because an empress rules over an entire empire,
with lots of different countries in it.
Actually, empires are a big reason languages
started dying out, my mother told me,
because everybody started speaking
the empire's language, instead of their own.)

The secret to an amazing pie, I learn,
is an amazing pie crust.

Some people believe in using lard,
which is pig fat, which sounds disgusting to me,
and fortunately sounds disgusting to Zoey, too.
Some people believe in using butter.
Some people believe in using vegetable shortening,
like Crisco, which comes in a can.

Zoey believes in using butter *and* shortening:
butter for the buttery flavor,
and shortening for the tender flaky texture.

I love watching Zoey use a pastry cutter
to chop the frozen butter and shortening
into tiny pieces, and then fold them
in with the flour, salt,
and *just* the right amount of water,
with her floury hands.

I love watching Zoey peel apples,
with the skin coming off in
perfect long spirals.

If Zoey decided to start a pie-baking club,
I would be the first one to sign up for it,
whether Lizard wanted to sign up for it or not.

After We Eat Super-Duper, Mega-Delicious Slices of Apple Pie Warm from the Oven

"You can take the rest of it home with you,"
Zoey offers.

Hooray!

"Give some to Lizard!"
Zoey says.

Um . . . maybe not?

So I guess Zoey,
who is so good
at noticing
so many things,

doesn't notice

everything.

When I Get Home

I wait for my mother to admire the freshly baked pie
(minus two pieces) sitting on the kitchen counter
with its flaky, tender, golden crust
in lattice strips across the top
and the cinnamony juice of the apples
that bubbled through as it baked.

She doesn't even see it.

"I'm going to lie down for a while," she says,
the minute she comes in the door from work.
"Can you find something in the fridge
you can have for your dinner?"

This time she looks so awful,
so pale and drained and sad,
that I can't not ask her,
"What's wrong, Mom?"

At first, I think she's not going to tell me.

But then she does.

"I didn't get the grant.

Apparently recording dying languages
before they go extinct is a low funding priority right now,
given agency budget cuts. After all, if one
more language is lost forever, who cares?"

Lizard and I do!

But anything I say will only make it worse.

So I have another slice of deep-dish apple pie
and a glass of milk for dinner,

all by myself.

When My Dad Calls That Night

He calls me on my phone,
since he tells me Mom didn't answer hers.

When I tell him about the grant, he says,
"Oh, no."

Then he says,
"This is really bad."

Then he says,
"Maybe I should come home early."

Then he says,
"But I can't. I really can't."

Then he says,
"But this is bad, honey."

Then he says,
"This is really, really bad."

Saturday Morning

I walk over to Lizard's house
after eating breakfast alone.

What if my mother never
comes out of her room again?

I'm still afraid Lizard might be mad
that I baked the pie with Zoey.

But once we're in the clubhouse, I tell her Mom's bad news,
and right away she turns back into the best friend ever.

"Your poor mom! This is so unfair! Someday, Bumble,
you and I are going to have a million dollars.

No, ten million, and *we'll* be the ones giving out the grants,
and we'll call ours the Lizard-and-Bumble Grant for Saving

Endangered Languages, and we'll give it all to your mom!
But you know what we should be doing now, right?

Even if Zari, Veronica, and Zoey have abandoned us?
And even if nobody—as in *nobody*—came to our club?

You and I can keep learning all the Guernésiais we can.
We can learn more and more. We can learn faster and faster.

There's still *us*, Bumble.
There's still *us*."

While We Practice Our Guernésiais

Lizard tells me every bad thing she knows about Zoey.
You may remember that Lizard is always the first one
to know anything bad about anybody.

Now she tells me that Zoey wet her pants in kindergarten,
which is something girls hardly ever do,
because boys are always the ones who are pants-wetters.

Plus she tells me that Zoey was the worst one
of anybody in the tap-dancing camp,
and everyone in the camp knew that except for Zoey.

Well, so what? I want to say. *Maybe some people get too scared
to ask to go to the bathroom and aren't good at tap dancing.
Maybe they're good at baking pies. And good at being friends.*

When I Get Home

Mom has come out of her room.
Down deep I knew she would.
She's still my *mom*.
Moms can't leave their kids *forever*.

In the Kitchen

My mom has Indian butter chicken
simmering on the stove in its spicy deliciousness.

"Where did the pie come from?" she asks.

"I baked it. With Zoey."

"I couldn't resist having a slice," she says.
"Honey, that Zoey is a *fabulous* baker."

She looks so happy that I feel guilty
for thinking I didn't want to tell her
about my deepening friendship with Zoey.

Because right now all I want—
all I want—
is to make my mother happy.

But Then That Evening

She doesn't eat the butter chicken
and brown rice with me.

And when she talks to my dad
behind the closed door of her room,
I can hear what sounds like crying.

One Huge Thing My Mother and Lizard Have in Common

They both never cry.

The Biggest Cryer in Our Family

My dad cries at the end of movies, not just sad movies,
but all movies, especially old Christmas movies,
like *Miracle on 34th Street* and *It's a Wonderful Life.*

He cries at the end of the final World Series game,
when the last out happens, and the crowd goes wild,
and the players practically knock each other down with hugs.

He cries during TV commercials, like the one
for some kind of batteries when the soldier dad comes home
and his little girl sees him and shouts, "Daddy!"

Most of all he cries for anything that has to do with me.
Piano recitals. Elementary school graduation.
The time I was in the third-grade spelling bee.

I know that when I sing the *Alice in Wonderland*
mean flower song, wearing my yellow rose costume,
there will be one person there blubbering his eyes out:

my dad.

Unlike My Dad

I don't cry about happy things. I mean,
why would you cry about something happy?

And when I cry about sad things,
I try not to do it in front of my mom,

so she won't say, "Oh, Betsy,"
the way she says, "Oh, James."

This is why I'm glad
I have Pooh Bear.

Not a Disney Pooh Bear
because I told you my mom hates Disney,

but the Pooh from the Ernest H. Shepard illustrations
in the books by A. A. Milne.

I can hold him tight all alone in my bed,
and he lets me cry as much as I want.

The way I did, a little bit, on the day I found out
I was going to be an extra flower instead of Alice.

Or the way I did, a lot, last night,
when my mom was in her room with the door shut,

and my dad was in North Carolina,
two thousand miles away,

so busy calming down my mom
that I didn't get my turn on the phone with him,

so there was just me and Pooh,
Pooh and me, crying together.

Sunday Morning without My Dad Is Awful, Too

I can't climb into my parents' big bed to wait
for someone to bring my mom and me Belgian waffles
with fresh strawberries and homemade whipped cream
and coffee for her and hot chocolate for me.

My mom sits hunched over her computer,
furiously writing another grant application for a deadline
early next week, one she didn't bother to apply for before,
because she thought she'd get the one she didn't get.

When I poke my head into her office door,
she waves me away without even saying good morning,
which of course it isn't.

I would have gone over to Lizard's,
but she texts me not to come.
She doesn't even say why, which is very strange.
But then she texts me again and says,
"My dad is sick."

Does she mean,
My dad is too hungover
for you to come?

Sunday morning used to be the best time of the week,
and now it's the worst, thanks to two dads.

And one mom.

Then I Surprise Myself

I text Zoey.
"Can I come over?

It's not too far
for me to ride my bike."

And she texts me
a thumbs-up emoji.

And an emoji picture
of a tiny pie.

Chocolate Cream Pie This Time

"Do you bake a pie every single day?"
I ask Zoey.

She laughs.
"No! We'd weigh five hundred pounds!"

While we work on the pie, I consider
telling her about my mother
and the grant, and how my dad's away
just when we need him most.

But the hard thing
about getting closer to somebody is
you have to tell them so much
about what happened *before*
for them to understand why you care so much
about what is happening *now*.

So we just talk about the play,
and how amazing Zari is as the Queen of Hearts
and how the girl who plays Alice is amazing, too.

"Much better than we would have been,"
Zoey says, and I don't mind that she said *we*
because it's true.

"Better than Veronica would have been, too,"
I add, "even though she's—"

"Seen the Disney movie fifteen times,"
Zoey says, finishing the sentence with me.

And we laugh, and the chocolate cream pie
is just as delicious as the deep-dish apple pie.

Baking a pie, it turns out, makes
an awful day a lot less awful.

More about the Chocolate Cream Pie

It's almost a relief to be at school on Monday.

Until lunch.

From her insulated lunch bag, Zoey pulls out
a plastic container with a huge slice
of chocolate cream pie and five plastic forks.

"Ta-da! Betsy and I baked this yesterday,
and I thought everybody would like to have some!"

Zari eats a big mouthful of pie right away.
"Wow!" she tells us.

"Yum! This is sooooo fabulous!" Veronica gushes,
through her second ginormous bite.

Lizard doesn't say anything.
Lizard doesn't pick up a fork.
Lizard doesn't take a single nibble.

Zoey looks worried.
"Are you allergic to chocolate?" she asks.
"Betsy and I could have baked a different kind
of pie if I had known."

"Yes," says Lizard,
who adores chocolate
and would eat it
every minute
of every day
if she could.

"Yes, I am."

As Soon as Lunch Is Over

Lizard pounces on me as we leave the cafeteria.
"Well, that didn't take long," she says.

"*What* didn't take long?" I ask,
but I already know the answer.

"My father is sick for *one* day, and
in *one* day you find yourself a new best friend."

"A person can have more than
one friend," I make myself say.

It occurs to me that this actually true,
even though I hadn't quite realized it before.

Besides, baking two pies with someone
doesn't exactly make them your best friend.

Though right now I think how restful it would be
to be best friends with Zoey rather than Lizard,

who bosses me around all the time,
and criticizes me all the time,

and makes me spend all my time practicing Guernésiais,
when she only knows about dying languages because of me.

"Be best friends with whoever
you want to, *Betsy*," Lizard says.

So I guess I'm not Bumble anymore?
I blink back the tears that start to well up.

"Bake a hundred pies if you want!" Lizard shouts.
"Bake a thousand pies! Bake a million!"

She whirls around and runs away from me,
her long black hair streaming behind her.

My Mom and Her Terrible, Horrible, No Good, Very Bad Day*

I'm too mad at Lizard
to meet her at her locker after school.

She's too mad at me
to meet me at mine.

Fine!

So I walk home to what was supposed to be
an empty house, but instead my mom is there.

She stayed home from the university to try to finish
the grant application, and she worked on it all day,

but somehow it vanished from her computer
just as she was about to press SEND.

She spent two hours on the phone
with the university tech person,

and he couldn't figure out how to get it back,
either, so now it's gone forever,

and she has to start the whole thing
all over again, but the deadline is tomorrow,

not that it matters, because she has a zero
chance of getting that grant anyway, and she can't

believe she's spent her whole professional life
doing something that the whole rest of the world thinks

is

worthless.

*When I was little, Mom read a book to me called *Alexander and the Terrible, Horrible, No Good, Very Bad Day*. It's as if she could already see this day coming.

Just Then

The doorbell rings.
It's Lizard.

"Great!" my mother says
under her breath.

And it strikes me how often
people say "Great!"

when they mean precisely
the opposite.

When Lizard Comes In

Lizard's cheeks are flushed,
and her breath comes hard and fast.

Because she ran all the way here?
Because she was—almost—crying?

Because she's sorry that she was so awful to me,
when it isn't a crime for me to have other friends?

She looks at me as if she might be going to apologize,
which is *not* Lizard's favorite thing to do.

In fact, I can't think of a single time
Lizard ever apologized to me about anything.

But then she notices my mom
standing in the doorway to the kitchen.

Her eyes dart from me,
to my mother,

and back to me,
then back to my mother again.

And I know that the last person in the world
Lizard wants to be wrong in front of is my mom,

who always thinks Lizard is wrong
about so many things already.

Instead of Apologizing to Me

Lizard straightens her shoulders.
Lizard draws herself up taller.

I can see her taking a deep breath,
her dark eyes shining with excitement.

And suddenly I know exactly
what she is going to say instead.

Lizard's Words Come Pouring Out

"Bumble told me you didn't get your grant,
which is so unfair—those jerks!
And I know you feel terrible—
of course you feel terrible!
All those languages that need saving!
And nobody else who cares!
So you have to save them all by yourself,
and those losers won't even give you
the money you need to do it!
So Bumble and I have a surprise for you,
which we were going to wait to tell you later,
but I think we need to tell you today.

We're saving a language, too!
It's called Guernésiais!
It's the language people used to speak
on the Isle of Guernsey,
and it's going extinct now,
so she and I are starting to speak it
to each other so we can keep it
from being lost forever,
sort of like what you're doing,
with the languages you write about!

And because you didn't get your grant,
now we're going to work
extra hard to save our language
by trying to speak it as much as we can,
even though nobody else
wants to speak it with us.

So we want you to know
that you don't have
to do this
all alone!"

As Lizard Is Talking

Suddenly I remember the cat we had once,
a long time ago,
when I was in fourth grade.

She was just with us for two months,
and then my mother decided that
the cat "wasn't working out."

The cat loved my mother best.
I've heard cats always love best
whoever loves them the least.

Blackie would kill mice and baby birds,
and she'd offer them to my mother
as her most precious gifts.

My mother would shudder and gag
and tell my dad, "Take it away, James.
Please. Please. Just take it away."

I look over at Lizard right now
beaming about how happy our project
is going to make my mother,

and somehow I have a terrible feeling
this is going to be like Blackie the cat
all over again.

"Is this some kind of joke?"

That's what my mother says.

"Are you two kidding me?"

That's what my mother says,
and now it's more like my mom
is Blackie the cat,
and Lizard is the soon-to-be-eaten mouse
and I'm the soon-to-be-eaten baby bird.

"A language is a living, breathing thing!"

That's what my mother says.
"It's the heart of a culture.
It's the soul of an entire way of life.
The languages I study
are the lifeblood of actual human beings,
usually Indigenous people,
who have already lost their *land*
to invasion
and colonization
and capitalism
and globalization
and the wickedness of sheer greed,
and now they're losing their *language*, too.
These are people
who are losing
everything!

This is an unspeakable human tragedy, girls!
This is not a *game*!"

The Whole Time My Mom Is Talking

I can't make myself look at Lizard.

But now I do.

My friend
who never ever cries

is crying.

Between Choking Sobs

"We—were—just—trying—to—help!"
Lizard gasps.
"We—even—made—a—club—
and advertised it with fifty posters—
and had special refreshments—
and decorations—
but—nobody—came."

Her face is twisted.
Tears are streaming from her eyes.
Snot is streaming from her nose.

"We've—been—practicing—so—hard—
even—though—no—one—else—would—
do—it—with—us!
Veronica—and Zoey—and Zari—
none of them cared about it—
nobody cared but us!"

She isn't even bothering
to wipe the tears and snot away.

Lizard forces the words out:
"This wasn't a *game*!
It wasn't a game to *me*!"

I Can Tell My Mother Feels Terrible Now

"Lizard, Lizard,
don't cry like that—
you'll make yourself sick.
Lizard, it's all right.
I didn't mean for
my tone
to be so harsh.
It's just that
no language
can be saved
by having
two people
who aren't part of
that *community,*
that *culture,*
that *tradition,*
that *history,*
learn a few words
to say to each other
once in a while,
thousands of miles away
from the land
and the people
whose language
this is.
I can see now
that you were just
trying to help.
But that's not
how a language *works.*"

But Everything She Is Saying Is Just Making It Even Worse

"I get it!" Lizard says,
and she's shouting now.

"I get that you think this was dumb.
I get that you think this was worthless.
I get that you never wanted
Bumble to be friends with me anyway.
I get that you're probably thrilled
she's best friends with Zoey now.

Once someone *gets* something,
you don't have to keep saying it
over and over and over again.

I GET IT!"

Lizard Storms Out the Door

I run after her.

I have to tell her
that I hate my mom now
for making my best friend cry.

I have to tell her
that I'm proud she and I
tried to save a dying language,
even if this was as pointless
as my mom said it was.

Maybe my mother's work
is pointless, too.

After all,
when a language is lost,
it's lost.

Who cares
what a dead language was like
when it was living?

What I Can't Help Believing

Pointless things
can still be worth doing.

Sometimes the point
is just how hard
you tried to do them.

Even if nobody else cared,
sometimes the point
is just how much
you cared.

There are so many things
I need to tell Lizard
if I can find the words
to say them.

When I Catch Up with Lizard

She leaps in before I can say
a single thing.

"*You're* the one who said,
Let's make this a surprise.

You're the one who said,
Let's make a club.

You're the one who told me
about dying languages in the first place.

You knew all along how horrible
this was going to be.

And you let me
do it anyway.

So I hope
you're happy now!

I hope you like being a dumb
extra flower in a dumb play!

I hope you like baking dumb
pies with dumb Zoey!

I hope you enjoy the dumb
rest of your dumb life!"

When she runs away this time,
I don't try to follow her.

When a language is lost,
it's lost.

Once a friendship is lost,
I guess it's lost, too.

Needless to Say

My mother spends the evening in her room, alone.
I spend the evening in my room, alone.

When I hear Dad's ringtone through her closed door,
she doesn't answer it.

When I hear his ringtone on my cell phone,
I don't answer it, either.

When he texts me,
"Is everything okay, honey?"
I don't text back.

When he leaves a voicemail,
"Please call, sweetie,"
I turn off my phone instead.

Sometimes you're too sad
even to talk to the person
who might make you less sad.

Tonight
is one of those
times.

When I Wake Up the Next Day

My mom is still in her room.
I tap softly on her door,
but she doesn't answer,
so I make my own breakfast.

I thought maybe she'd come out
before I left for school
to make sure I didn't forget anything,
or to tell me to have a good day.

But she doesn't,
and I know not to bother her
when she's behind that closed door.

Lizard and I don't meet at our lockers before the first bell.

We don't whisper to each other
in science or math class.

At lunch, we let the others talk about the play.

Zoey catches my eye and mouths to me,
"Is something wrong?"

I shake my head,
and I know she knows
that *everything* is wrong,
but I can't talk about it now,
and I can't talk about it later, either.

So at rehearsal
the only thing she asks me
is what kind of pie
I want to bake next.

The Best Surprise Ever

When I walk home from school after play rehearsal,
I open the front door, and guess who I see?

"Daddy!"

I hurl myself into his arms,
and I hug him and hug him and hug him,
and he hugs me and hugs me and hugs me.

"You came back early!"

"I missed you both too much," he says,
his voice choked up
with the force of all that missing.
"Being away for a week is one thing,
but two weeks? That's just too long."

I don't remind him that Mom's research trips
often last a month or more,
because I'm just so happy he's home.

"Daddy, promise me you'll never go away again."

He says, "I promise."

"Cross your heart and hope to die?"

He crosses his heart,
and then he hugs me again,
as if he's never going to get me go.

My Dad Can Fix Anything

He can patch a flat tire.
Unclog a bathroom drain.
Make that grinding sound stop on the disposal.
Unjam the printer.
Sew a button eye onto a teddy bear.
Get the junk drawer open when it's stuck.
Bang out a dent on the garage door.
Superglue broken dollhouse furniture.
Repair the motor on the ceiling fan.
Patch a torn window screen.
Bandage a sprained ankle.
Mend a ripped seam in a favorite T-shirt.
Kiss a boo-boo and make it better.

Now that he's home again
maybe he can fix everything
for my mom and Lizard and me.

Everything Is So Wonderful Now

"When is Mom getting home from work?"
I ask him.
"Does she know you're here,
or is this a surprise for her, too?"

"Well, that's actually the main reason
I came back early," he says.

"A keynote speaker for a major linguistics conference
had to cancel at the last minute,
so the conference organizers begged your mom
to fly out today to take his place."

He looks uncomfortable when he says this,
as if I'll mind that the main reason he changed his plans
wasn't because of how much he missed me.

But I don't mind a bit.

"Wow!" I say.
"Will this make Mom feel better
about—you know—the grant thing?"

"I hope so, sweetie," he says,
and his voice cracks again.
"God, I hope so."

It feels like a freaky miracle:

my mom is totally depressed about her life
one minute,
and then the next minute,
she's flying off to be the star
of a fancy conference.

Even though my dad had nothing to do
with Mom getting this cool invitation,
somehow it feels as if
he's starting to fix things
for Mom and me
already.

At My Locker the Next Morning

Lizard comes up to me.
She doesn't say anything about
the terrible, horrible, no good, very bad day.
She acts like it never happened.

I'm so glad she's there at my locker again
in the old best-friend way,
that it's completely fine with me
to act like it never happened, too.

It almost feels to me
like it was a terrible dream:
my mom not getting the grant,
my mom freaking out about her computer,
my mom yelling at Lizard,
my mom making Lizard cry.

Now that my dad is home,
the world—well, my world—
feels like it's back to normal.
My mom is off on a great work trip,
and Lizard is here at my locker,
like any ordinary Wednesday morning.

"I heard your dad is home," she says.

How could Lizard possibly know this,
even if she's the one who knows everything?

"Your dad told my mom,"
Lizard explains.

That's kind of weird.
It's not like our parents ever hang out together.
They chat pleasantly at school events,
but that's about it.
My dad must be so happy about my mom's big honor
that he wants to tell the whole world.

"Yes!" I say. "He got back last night!"
Fizzy happiness bubbles up in me again.

She looks as if she's about to say something else,
but then the bell rings,
and the only reason I know
that all the bad stuff really did happen
is that this time Lizard didn't say
"Good morning" to me
in Guernésiais.

The Other Way I Know That All the Bad Stuff Really Did Happen

Lizard is awfully quiet later on
as we meet in the hall before science class,
and when we walk from science to math,
and when we're in the locker room getting changed for PE.
She's awfully quiet all day.

It's like there is something she wants to say
but doesn't.

If I were Lizard,
which I'm not,
what I would want to say is
I'm sorry for shouting
all those terrible things!

But you already know
that *I'm sorry*
is not Lizard's favorite thing to say.

So I'm awfully quiet all day, too.
Even though Lizard and I
acted like nothing had happened
when we chatted for two minutes at her locker
before the first bell,
I know that if we really started talking,
the way we always talked before,
it would be hard to keep pretending.

So at her locker after school, I just say,
"I need to go home to spend time with my dad.
You know, because he was away so long."

And all Lizard says is
"Cool."

She opens her mouth
as if to say something else.

Then she closes it again.

A Perfect Evening

My dad and I make plain old spaghetti for dinner
and leave the dirty pots in the sink.
"To soak," he says.
Something that would never happen
if my mom were here.

I don't practice piano.
"It's fine to miss a day every once in a while,"
he tells me.

We stream the Disney *Alice in Wonderland*,
which I've never seen even once,
let alone fifteen times.
My dad sings along
to the White Rabbit's song
about being late, late, late,
for a very important date.

I love my dad so much!
I love my mom, too (of course).

But my mom and I have never had
an evening as perfect,
just the two of us,
as this perfectly ordinary evening
for just my dad and me.

At the Lunch Table on Thursday

When I arrive at the lunch table on Thursday
a couple of minutes late because
Mrs. Oliphant kept us past the bell in language arts,
Lizard is talking about something
to Zoey, Zari, and Veronica

in a low, earnest voice,
as if the four of them have been best friends
since third grade, instead of her and me.
But she isn't close friends with any of them,
the way I'm starting to be with Zoey now.

It must be something to do with me
because she breaks off abruptly
when I reach the table.

And when I sit down in my usual seat
I'm the one whose eyes she's avoiding.

Now It's Zoey's Turn to Avoid My Eyes

At rehearsal Zoey is quieter than usual.

"What's your *favorite* pie?" she finally asks.
I can tell she's just asking this
to make conversation, not because
she really wants to know.

I shrug. "Maybe deep-dish apple pie?
Or chocolate cream?"

She laughs because it's obvious I picked these
because they're the two pies we made together.
But her laugh is more like a nervous giggle.

"What about you? What's your favorite pie?"
But I don't really want to know, either.

I thought she and I were going to become true friends,
but this won't happen if the only thing
we talk about anymore is pie.

Plus, it's strange how she won't look straight at me,
and how she keeps twisting her hands in her lap.

"What's going on?" I ask. "It's Lizard, right?
She told you something bad about me, right?"

"Oh, Betsy," Zoey says. "She told us
what happened to your mom."

I Stare at Zoey

I can't figure out what on earth
she's talking about. Well, okay,
I guess I can, but why on earth
would Lizard share this with the others?

Unless she was explaining why she doesn't
want to be friends with me anymore, after all?
I'm so confused that the words
come pouring out of me in a rush.

"*What* happened to my mom?
That she didn't get her grant?
And had this big huge meltdown?
And it was horrible?

I mean, it really was horrible,
and Lizard saw the whole thing,
but I'm pretty sure everything
is going to be better now.

My mom got invited to this big-deal
conference, so that will cheer
her up, and my dad's home now
from his own big-deal trip.

You haven't met my dad yet,
but when he's around,
everything gets better
all the time for everyone.

So I don't know why Lizard
even told you this."

What Zoey Says

I expect to see Zoey's face light up with relief
that the bad thing Lizard told her about my mom
ended up being
not so terrible.

But instead her face looks like
the face in this famous picture
of a person screaming
on a bridge somewhere—
wide eyes and open mouth,
maybe not screaming out loud,
but a silent scream,
like when you're in a bad
dream and you're trying
to call for help
and no sound comes out.

She puts her hand on my arm,
and says,
"I didn't realize—
Lizard didn't tell us that—
I thought you already knew—"

And then in my heart
I do know

now.

Mr. Delgado Claps His Hands

"Flowers! Up on stage!
We're already running late today!
Girls, it's time for singing,
not time for gabbing.
You two in the back—
Zoey, Betsy—yes,
I'm talking to you!"

Instead of Going Up on Stage

Without a word,
I break free from Zoey.

I race out the rear door
of the auditorium.

Dad answers his phone
on the first ring.

"What's going on with Mom really?
Why didn't you tell me?"

We Are Sitting on the Couch in the Family Room

He's on one end.
I'm on the other.

I tried to make him tell me everything
before I would even get in the car.

But he said, "Not here, honey.
We can't talk here."

When we got home, he wanted me
to sit right next to him,

so he could pull me close to him
and hold me while we talked.

But I said,
"No. I want to sit *here*."

So I'm as far away from him on the couch
as he is from me in my heart.

Here's What I Find Out

She's in the hospital,
but she's awake now.

She took sleeping pills.
A lot of them.

That's why I didn't see her
Tuesday morning.

When neither of us
answered our phones

on that bad night,
or returned his messages,

Dad canceled everything
for the rest of his trip

and caught the next
flight home.

Then while I was at school
he found her and called 911.

He told Lizard's mom
what happened

because he thought
she should know

to give me some extra
love right now.

He would never have told her
if he'd thought she'd tell Lizard.

The Person My Dad Didn't Tell

My dad didn't tell me.
He didn't tell his own daughter.

He told Lizard's mother,
and she told Lizard,
and Lizard told Zoey,
and Zoey told me.

But my dad
lied to me.

My dad
lied to me.

The First Three People I Hate Right Now

My mother:
What kind of mother
would try to leave her husband and her daughter,
would leave my *father* and *me*,
forever—FOREVER,
because she didn't get a stupid *grant*?
Because she lost a file on her stupid *computer*?

Lizard:
What kind of best friend,
even if she turned
into a former best friend,
wouldn't tell *me*
that something this horrible had happened,
but would tell *three* other people instead,
so all of them could share a secret—
my family's secret—
and I'd be the only one left out?

Zoey:
It's not her fault
that she had to be the one
to let me know
the happy things I was thinking
were totally fake.
But it's hard
not to hate her
for it a little bit
anyway.

The Person I Hate Most of All

My father:
Why did he even agree to go on that trip?

Why did he think he had to spend
a whole week in the Smoky Mountains
just to make some guy's fancy furniture?

Why did he plan to stay an extra week
to help some old lady
(whom I've never even met)
fix up her falling-down house,
and not even care
that everything in *our* house
would fall apart while he was away?

Why did he make up a stupid story
about how my mother had been
invited to that huge important fabulous conference?

Why did I let myself
be dumb enough to believe him?

I'll tell you why:

He was the one person in the world
I could trust completely.

He was the one person in the world
I could always count on.

He was the one person in the world
who loved me so much
he would tell me the truth,
no matter what.

He was all of these things,
until I found out

he wasn't

any of them.

What I Want to Ask My Dad

"Why did you lie to me?"

But how can I know
that whatever he says in reply

won't just be another lie?

But I Have to Ask Him Anyway

He says:

"I just couldn't bear
for you to know.

All I've ever wanted
is for you to be safe and happy.

And I read that kids—
even kids your age—

sometimes . . . harm themselves . . .
because they know someone else

who did it . . .
or tried to do it . . .

like someone else at school . . .
or a friend . . .

or most of all . . .

a parent.

And if anything ever happened to you,

Betsy, honey, if anything ever happened to you . . .

I couldn't go on living myself

if anything ever happened to you."

Then I Have to Ask My Dad, Even Though I'm Afraid to Hear the Answer

"Why did Mom do it?"

What Dad Tells Me

"Your mother has been struggling
with depression and anxiety
for a long time, honey.

And this week, with me away,
it just became more
than she could handle.

When people are in that dark place,
they can't think clearly.

She said she thought
we'd be better off without her.

She said she ruins everything
when she's around.

She said the two of us are happier
when she's away on a trip.

She said she thought it would be
a good thing if this time
she went away

and didn't come back."

The Worst Part

The thing I feel most terrible about?

I have thought those exact same things.

My mom ruined our project to save
our endangered language.
My mom made my best friend cry.
My mom made Lizard feel
like she's the wrong friend for me.
Sometimes my mom makes me feel
like I'm the wrong daughter for her.

Everything *is* more fun
when my mom's away on a trip.
Just yesterday
I was thinking how perfect it was
to have her gone,
so that it was just my dad and me.

I feel sick inside right now
that I actually did spend the whole evening,
just yesterday,
thinking these things,

while she was in the hospital

because she tried to kill herself,

because

she thought

I thought

I'd be better off

without her.

My Biggest Question

"So what happens now?"
I ask my dad.

"She'll stay at the hospital for a while.
I don't know how long.
Of course, she's begging them
to let her come home now
so she won't have to miss
any more classes at the university.
But her doctor told her,
'If you were badly injured in a car accident,
you wouldn't be at the university
teaching your classes right now,
and this is as every bit as serious as that.'

The doctor will help her
find the right medication
to manage her dark moods,
and a therapist to talk to
about what happened
and how to make sure
it won't happen again.

I hope that
what happens now
is that things
will get better
for her,
for you,
for me,
for all of us."

I'm Still Stunned

I can hardly think.
I can hardly feel.

I can hardly believe
this started out
like a normal day:
with Lizard meeting me at my locker,
the way she did the day before
when I was so relieved that
we could still
be friends again;
with Zoey sitting next to me
at another flower rehearsal,
asking me a nice boring question,
like "What's your favorite pie?"

Right now
I can't believe
I'll ever have
a normal day
ever again.

Before I Go to Bed That Night

My father says I don't have to go to school tomorrow.

He says he's going to call the guidance counselor
and tell her what happened.
He'll call Mr. Delgado, too,
so he won't be mad at me
for leaving rehearsal early.

But I tell my dad I don't mind going to school.
Even if nothing will ever be normal again,
I want to be able to pretend it is,
at least a little tiny bit.

It's easier to pretend,
if I'm watching a film about the ancient Mayans
in social studies,
or talking about perspective in art,
or taking a grammar quiz in language arts,

than if I'm sitting at home on a school day,
just my dad and me,

knowing why
it's just my dad and me.

The Person Who Is Always the First One Who Knows Everything

That person must know
I'm never going to speak to her
ever again.

She must know
you can't take the worst thing
that ever happened to your best friend
and tell it to everyone else
except her.

She must know
some things
can never be forgiven.

She must know
this thing
is one of

those things.

What I Can See When I Close My Eyes

I picture her
sitting there at the lunch table,
thrilled that she had the absolute
worst bad thing ever
about me to tell them,
lowering her voice
so they'd have to lean in to hear,
waiting for how shocked and sad
they'd be, but all of them
relieved that this happened
to someone else

and not
to them.

Things That Don't Surprise Me

I'm not surprised
Lizard doesn't meet me at my locker
before school on Friday.

I'm not surprised
when Ms. Prakash asks us
to pick lab partners in science
for the unit on electromagnetism,
and Lizard doesn't even look my way,
so I end up with a boy I barely know.

I'm not surprised
we sit like strangers in math
in our side-by-side seats,
where we will be sitting
side by side until May,
because in Mr. J's class,
wherever you sit on the first day
of school is your assigned seat
for the rest of the year,
to make it easier for him
to learn our names,
which he keeps forgetting
anyway.

We sit like strangers,
as Mr. J starts to write
equations on the board
that I can hardly read
because my eyes are
blurry with tears,

as it occurs to me
that if Lizard could have done
that unforgivable thing,
maybe the two of us
were strangers
all along.

What Does Surprise Me

Lizard isn't at our table at lunch.

"Where's Lizard?"
I ask the others.

A long, uncomfortable pause follows
as they look at one another with twitchy eyes.

Maybe I shouldn't have sat here
for lunch today, either.

Maybe lunch is one more thing
that can never be normal for me again.

Veronica is the first one to answer:
"When Zoey told us
that you didn't know about . . ."
Her voice trails off.

Zari takes over:
"Well, when we found out that
Lizard told it to us
when she hadn't even told it
to you . . ."

Zoey finishes:
"The three of us told her
she couldn't sit with us
at lunch anymore."

Veronica says,
"I mean, who wants to sit
with someone who's a—"

The three of them say it together:
"Traitor."

For Some Reason I Have to Ask the Next Question

"But where *is* Lizard?"

The three of them shrug,
as if they have no interest whatsoever
in the whereabouts of traitors.

I shouldn't care, either.
But caring about somebody
isn't something you can just turn off,
like a faucet.

It's more like a leaky faucet,
where you turn the handle as tight as you can—
righty tighty, lefty loosey—
but there is that little
drop-drop-drop
that keeps on dripping.

It isn't as if there is
any other place Lizard can be.

Unless she's in the bathroom?
But there are teachers who stand in the hall
to make sure no one at Southern Peaks
spends too long in the bathroom
because last year some eighth graders
spent too long in the bathroom
and it turned out to be something
that had to do with drugs.

I peer around the cafeteria.
But it isn't as if Lizard has any other real friends.
She just had me,
and I just had her,
except now I have Zoey, too.

Now Lizard doesn't have me,
and I don't have her,
and we're never going
to have each other again.

And without me,
and without Zari, Zoey, and Veronica,
now Lizard doesn't have
anywhere to sit
at all.

Then I See Her

She's sitting at the table where
the Spanish-speaking kids always sit together.

Maybe she did decide to try to learn Spanish,
now that she's given up on saving Guernésiais?

Or maybe she's sitting there just because
there was an open spot at that table?

Or maybe this is her way
of sitting alone,
but not alone.

The Spanish-speaking kids
aren't going to stop speaking Spanish
just because some uninvited kid
plopped herself down at their table.

So Lizard's not going to be able to talk to them,
and they're not going to want to talk to her.

Maybe she thought it was time
for her to spend an entire lunch period
without lecturing anybody
or bossing anybody
or making anybody

feel bad about anything.

Mom's Coming Home on Monday

That's what my dad tells me
after he visits her on Saturday morning.

The other times he visited her,
I was at school or rehearsal.
This time I was right here at home.
But I didn't ask to go with him.
Even before my father told me,
"This isn't a place for kids,"
I already knew that.

It's not like I need Lizard,
or anybody else,
to tell me *everything*.

No Welcome Signs This Time

When my mom would come home
from one of her research trips,
my dad and I would make big signs.

His would say, WELCOME HOME, KATHLEEN!

Mine would say, WELCOME HOME, MOM!
with each letter written with a different-colored marker,
and drawings of
hearts,
flowers,
smiley-faced suns,
shooting stars,
fireworks,
ice cream cones,
and rainbows.

This time neither of us
suggest making any
huge welcome-home banners.

This wasn't that kind of a trip.
This isn't that kind of a homecoming.

Confession

I have to admit
I don't know what I feel
about my mom coming home.

I don't know what I feel
about my mom,
period.

Part of me feels terrible
that she somehow knew
I really am happier
a lot of the time
when she's not here.

But part of me feels angry
that she's the kind of mom
who is so tense
and stressed
and anxious
and depressed

that she'd make
her kid feel happier
when she's gone.

Part of me feels even angrier
that she didn't care
how guilty I'd feel
for the rest of my life
if she left
forever.

Part of me feels desperately sad
that my mother was sad enough
to do this.
My father said depression and anxiety
are forms of mental illness,
and people shouldn't be blamed
for them any more
than they should be blamed
for getting cancer.

Part of me feels scared.
What will I say when I see her?
What will I do?
What will she say when she sees me?
What will she do?

There are so many different parts of me
feeling so many different things.

And all the different things
feel horrible.

The One Thing That All of Me Knows

I wouldn't be better off without my mom.

She lets me see there is a whole world out there
filled with people who speak different languages.

She shows me how important it is
to care about something bigger than yourself,
like studying dying languages
when they are still there to be studied.

She sees beauty in words.

She sees beauty in everything:
flowers
and classical music
and meals made from scratch
and eaten by candlelight.

She makes me practice the piano
so the rest of my life I can be grateful
that I know how to play Chopin
and Beethoven and Brahms.

She thinks I deserve to have a best friend
who doesn't try to control everything I do.

She is passionate about life

and intense

and super smart

and beautiful

and a great cook

and the best in our family at Scrabble.

Two More Reasons Why I Wouldn't Be Better Off without My Mom

She loves me.

And I love her.

Since Zoey Told Me That Terrible Thing

She has texted me a few times,
saying, "Are you okay?"

and "Is there anything I can do?"
and "Do you want to come over?"

I haven't texted her back.
No, I'm not okay.

No, there is nothing you can do.
No, I don't want to come over.

My mom once told my dad and me
about some king in ancient times

who got bad news about a battle,
or some kind of news like that.

He was so angry about the defeat
he killed the man who brought the message!

She said this is called "blaming the messenger,"
and people do it all the time,

even though it's completely unfair
to blame the poor messenger

for the content
of the message,

just the way I can't help
blaming Zoey for this one.

Flowers and Pie Instead

Maybe this isn't the kind of homecoming
where you make a sign.
But my mother said once,
when she and my father
were going to a dinner party
where the hostess said not to bring anything,
"It's always appropriate
to give flowers
or a bottle of wine."

When my mother comes home,
I'm not going give her
a bottle of wine.
Obviously!

But I can give her some flowers.
Maybe Zoey and I can bake her another pie.
She loved that deep-dish apple pie so much.
It was the one thing that made her happy
even after she didn't get the grant.
I couldn't resist having a slice.
Honey, that Zoey is a fabulous baker!

But first I have to make myself ask
that fabulous baker
(and bad-news messenger)
to bake it with me.

I Text Zoey to Ask Her

Zoey texts back, "YES!"

I text that it's for my mom,
who's coming home
from the hospital tomorrow,
and she texts a smiley face.

When my dad drops me off
at Zoey's house
on Sunday afternoon,
Zoey gives me the kind
of hug that says the things
it's hard to find the words to say.

"My mom loved that deep-dish apple pie,"
I tell her.

"Then let's get busy,"
Zoey says.

Zoey and I bake the pie together,
and it looks just as golden and glorious
as the first one did.

Maybe even better.

Because Zoey and I
are better friends now, too.

What Color Roses?

Zoey's mom drives me home afterward,
and Zoey comes along in the car.
I ask if we can make a quick stop
at King Soopers to get my mother some flowers.
I brought twenty dollars saved from my allowance
just in case.

"I'm going to get her red roses,"
I tell them.
"My mother told me that red is the color
for *passionate* love."

"Passionate doesn't mean
lots and lots of love,"
Zoey says.
"It means being *in* love.
You know, like . . ."
She makes a kissy face.

I guess all my best friends
do need to explain things to me.

Now I don't know what color roses to get.
Yellow is the cheeriest, but yellow roses
made my mother cry that other time when she thought
her boyfriend didn't love her the way she wanted him to.
That last thing I want is to make my mother cry.

So I buy an already-made bouquet of mixed flowers
of lots of different kinds and colors,
hoping she'll know it means
I'm feeling too many things
for any one kind or color of flower
to be able to express them all.

The Scariest Thing You'll Ever Have to Do

Walk home from school alone
because you no longer have a best friend
to walk with you.

Know that when you open the door
she is going to be there,

your mother who's coming home
from the hospital
after trying to kill herself.

Wonder what she's going to say to you.
Wonder what you're going to say to her,

your mother who spent her whole life
studying languages before they would be lost forever.

What language is there anywhere in the world
that would have the words for this?

If there ever was
such a language,

it has to be one
that got lost

a long,
long
time
ago.

I Make Myself Open the Door

I smell beef bourguignon in the oven.

                                               Beef bourguignon?

I hear Mozart's *Jupiter* Symphony
playing at full volume.

                                               Mozart?

Are we supposed to pretend
this never happened?

She comes out of the kitchen,
wiping her hands on a dish towel.
"Did you have a good day, honey?"

She is all smiles

until
she
sees
my
face.

Now All the Words I've Been Keeping Inside Come Rushing Out

"NO!"

My father is behind her,
shaking his head at me,
holding up both hands
as if he's a traffic cop
and I'm the speeding car
about to crash into the barricade.

"NO, I DID NOT HAVE A GOOD DAY!
I DID NOT HAVE A GOOD DAY
BECAUSE OF YOU!"

I can't stop now.
I'm a speeding car with no brakes.
I don't care if I crash into the barricade.
I want to smash it as hard as I can.
I want to smash it
into a million, billion, trillion pieces.

"I WILL NEVER HAVE A GOOD DAY AGAIN
BECAUSE OF YOU
AND HOW YOU TRIED TO LEAVE DAD AND ME
FOREVER!"

No More Barricade

Now she's holding me,
and my father is holding both of us.

I'm sobbing.
She's sobbing.

This time
my father is the only one
who isn't crying.

"I'm sorry,
I'm sorry,
I'm sorry,
I'm sorry,"

she sobs.

"Betsy,
my baby,
I'm sorry,
I'm sorry,
I'm sorry."

We Talk, and Talk, and Talk

We talk for hours, the three of us.
We almost forget to eat
the beef bourguignon,
until my father remembers it,
and then we eat it while sitting
in my parents' big bed upstairs
while we talk, and talk, and talk.

My mother didn't try to do this thing
because of not getting the grant,
or because of the thing that went wrong with her computer,
or even because of how she yelled at Lizard.

Though how she yelled at Lizard was a part of it.
Maybe everything was a part of it.

"I thought someone who could make
a child cry like that,
because she cared more about the importance
of her *work* than about a child's *feelings*
didn't deserve to live.

And—oh, honey—I was just so tired.
Tired of the bullies at the department meetings.
Tired of fighting nonstop with the people
I work with every day.
And your father was gone on that trip—
and I wanted him to go—it was his turn to go—
but it was just so hard having him gone,
and I hated myself for how I couldn't hold
it together without him for two measly weeks.

It was everything, honey, all of it,
the stress of everything put together.
I was just—so—tired."

My Voice Comes Out Very Small When I Ask This

"Were you tired—
of me—
too?"

"No!"

She's not crying now.
I'm not crying, either.
We used up all the tears inside of us,
even the ocean of extra-salty tears
that was building up inside of her
for years and years.

"I could never be tired of you!

But I was tired
of being so tired
of everything else
that I couldn't be the mother
I wanted to be.

I could *never* be tired of you
or of your father!

But when a person is
stressed
and depressed
and anxious
and tired,
deep in her bones,
in every fiber of her being,
it's hard to find
the energy
to be the person
she wants to be.

And I couldn't face
being
the person
I was."

There Is Something Else I Need to Know

"How are you going to stop being tired?"
I ask her.

"There are medications that help control
depression and anxiety.
I'm starting on one of them now,
but it can take a few weeks
before it starts to take effect.
I'm seeing a therapist to talk about
why I can't seem to let go
of the worries that stress me so much."

These are the things my father already told me,
but I needed to hear her say them, too.

"I'm taking a medical leave
for the rest of the semester,
and I'm going to have a lighter
teaching load in the spring.
I'm actually relieved now
that I didn't get the grant.
I can't keep driving myself
so hard to study every
dying language everywhere.

There are just too many
dying languages.

No one person
can do

everything."

This Time My Voice Starts Out Small, but Then It Gets Bigger

"Lizard and I
tried to help.

We were really, truly
just trying to help.

We picked a language,
with a red dot
on the dying languages map,
because we thought
it needed help
the most.

And we were so proud
of learning at least
a little bit of it,
and trying to speak it,
not only the two of us,
but we tried to get
Zari and Zoey and Veronica
to speak it at lunch
so they'd be part
of helping to save it, too,
and like Lizard said,
we tried to make a club,
but nobody came.
We tried so hard!

And you thought we were
doing it as a *joke*!

And that broke Lizard's heart."

What I Don't Go On to Say

And then Lizard broke my heart.

Even though Lizard and I aren't friends anymore,
and we will never be friends again,
I still don't want my mother
to think bad things about her.

I think maybe Lizard's heart
was breaking a little bit all along
because she couldn't help knowing
that her best friend's mother hated her.

My Mother and Lizard

"Why do you hate Lizard so much?"
I ask her,
since today seems to be the day
to ask every question
I've ever had about everything.

My mother stares at me.

"I don't hate Lizard!"

"Yes, you do.
You've hated her all along.
You know you have!"

"Honey, listen to me.
How could I hate Lizard?
It's true I haven't been thrilled
about how much she tries to dictate
everything the two of you do together,
as if her ideas and opinions
are the only ones that matter.
It's been hard for me to see
how she expects you to follow
her lead, all the time, everywhere.
But that's hardly the same thing
as *hating* someone.

Actually,
in many ways,
I admire Lizard
for being so spunky and spirited,
for how willing she is
to be herself,
always.
I truly do.

I just didn't want her to drain
all the spunk and spirit
out of you.

I didn't want Lizard
to take up so much space
in your friendship,

with Lizard
being Lizard,

that there wouldn't be
any room left

for you to be
Betsy."

I'm Done Talking for Now

So my mother doesn't hate Lizard.
She *admires* her.

Because Lizard has spunk and spirit.
And I don't.

Because Lizard is always Lizard, despite everything.
And I've never figured out how to be Betsy.

My Father's Turn to Talk

My father has been very quiet
for a long, long time.

For the last two hours—or three?—
he's just listened to my mother and me.

But we couldn't have done our talking,
if he hadn't been there doing his listening.

Now he reaches over
and takes my hand.

"Kathleen," he says,
"sometimes someone who is quiet

has their spunk and spirit
deep inside, like a hidden treasure.

They feel more deeply
and hurt more deeply

and love more deeply,
in ways the rest of us can't see.

Yes, Lizard is indeed
a force to be reckoned with.

But I'd put my money
on our Betsy, any day."

This Is Why I Love My Father More Than Anything

He sees more in me

than my mother does.

He sees more in me

than anyone else does.

He sees more in me

than I see in myself.

My Mother Takes My Other Hand

"James—
I didn't mean . . .

James, of course Betsy
has her own gifts.

I'd rather have her as my daughter
than any other child on earth.

I guess . . .
No, I know . . .

I haven't done
as good a job

as I should have
of showing that."

Now she turns
toward me

and looks
into my eyes

as if she's
really, truly

seeing me
for the first time.

"I haven't done
as good a job

as I should have
at so many things,

my precious,
my beautiful,

Betsy."

Now We Are Really Done Talking for Today

One time I asked my mother
how many words there are in the English language.

She said there is no easy way
to answer that question.

For one, it's hard to decide
what counts as a *word*,
because the same group of letters
can be a noun,
like *dog* is the name for an animal,
or a verb,
like *dog* means to follow persistently.
Plus there is the *dog* in *hot dog*,
where we could say,
"Put some more *dogs* on the grill."

For another, it's hard to decide
what counts as *English*,
because there are so many foreign words
that are part of English now
(like *taco* and *spaghetti*),
plus slang (which is always changing)
and regional dialects
and abbreviations
and more.

But then she said the answer
is around a quarter of a million.

I feel like we spoke
a quarter of a million words
tonight.

I Stay Home from School on Tuesday

This time when my father asks me
if I want to stay home from school for the day,
I say yes.

We go for a family bike ride on the creek path.
We curl up reading together in the family room.
We eat Zoey's deep-dish apple pie.

And we take an afternoon nap.

A long afternoon nap.

My mother isn't the only one
who is
just—
so—
tired.

My father and I are
just—
so—
tired,
too.

But after the bike ride,
and the reading,
and eating up every single crumb of the entire apple pie,
and the nap,
we are a lot less tired
than we were before.

There Is a New Topic of Conversation at the Lunch Table on Wednesday

Veronica has a crush on Trevor,
who is one of the playing cards in *Alice*.

She thinks he has a crush on her, too,
because he stopped horsing around
with the other playing cards
when Mr. Delgado called the flowers
up on the stage to practice their song yesterday
(at the rehearsal I missed
because of spending the day
with my parents),
and he stared at the flowers
for the whole time instead.

If Lizard was here,
she would say,

"What makes you think he's looking at *you*
and not at Rose, Larkspur, Daisy, or Violet?"

But Lizard isn't here.

Veronica Talks about Trevor for Ten Whole Minutes

Then Zari changes the subject.

"I heard Mr. Delgado telling one of the moms
that he's transferring to the high school next year."

"That can't be true!"
Veronica says.
"Why on earth would he want to teach
high school kids when he could be
teaching us?"

Zoey and I just shrug.
Zari shrugs, too.

If Lizard was here,
she would say
(at least under her breath to me),
"Hmm . . .
I wonder why . . .
Could it be that stuck-up flowers
get annoying after a while?"

But Lizard isn't here.

What Veronica Says Next

"Did you see that Lizard has started
sitting with the Mexican kids?"

"With the *Mexican* kids?"
Zari asks.

"Yes," Veronica says.
She inclines her head
in the direction of that table.
"Over there.
With the Mexican kids."

"You mean,
with the *American* kids?"
Zari asks.
"With the kids
who are just as American
as anyone else,
but who happen to prefer
speaking to each other
in Spanish?"

"Of course!"
Veronica said.
"You know that's
who I meant."

This is exactly the same thing
Lizard would have said,
if she was here.

But Lizard isn't here.

I Steal a Glance at Lizard across the Room

I wonder if she feels lonely there,
with everyone else speaking in Spanish,

a language she didn't want to learn
because hundreds of millions of people

already speak it, so Spanish didn't
need to be rescued by Lizard.

I wonder if Lizard misses me.
I wonder if I'm starting to miss Lizard.

But then, from across the room,
I hear her laugh at something funny

one of the other kids said.
Maybe Lizard does know Spanish now,

the way she always knows everything,
even the terrible thing about my mom

that she blabbed to everyone else,
but not to me.

What If I Marched Up to Lizard at Her Locker after School Today?

What if I said to Lizard
"How could you *do* that?

How could you tell *them*
about my mom, and not tell *me*?

Was it so important to be the one
who knows everything first,

that you had to show off
how you even knew this,

when poor, pitiful Bumble
(talk about a poor, pitiful nickname!)

didn't even know it yet?
Oh, and by the way,

how would you like it
if I told the others about your dad?

That he's not a spy
but an alcoholic?

How would you like it
if I was the important know-it-all now?"

But I Don't March Up to Lizard at Her Locker

I would never tell the others

about Lizard's father.

I would never do to her

what she did to me.

Instead

After school I head to our private clubhouse
to get the few things I keep there.

I don't want anything of mine
to be left behind with anything of hers.

I take a different route from the one
I used to walk with Lizard,

so she won't see me sneaking toward her house,
though if she does, I don't care.

I don't care what Lizard
thinks about anything anymore.

Things I Gather Up When I Get There

The little plastic Winnie-the-Pooh plate,
bowl, and cup I've had since I was a baby.

A notebook where I wrote poems
that only Lizard has ever read.

Plus my can of pencils,
which was just an empty soup can,

until Lizard helped me glue
a piece of fabric around it

that had pictures of flying geese,
like dreams winging through the sky.

I see the printout she made of
"Words and Phrases in Guernésiais,"

so I take that, too, even though
I could always print out another one,

if I ever needed it, which I won't,
as I now know what a dumb plan that was,

to think that two kids in Colorado
could save a dying language

on an island in the English Channel,
thousands of miles away.

But I want it anyway,
because it was the last thing

Lizard and I ever did together,
back when we were still

friends.

Lizard Is the One Who Should Be a Spy, Not Her Dad

She creeps up on me so quietly
I don't hear anything,

until suddenly I sense someone behind me,
and I whirl around,

and there she is.

Even if she wasn't talented at spying,
it's pretty obvious what I'm doing,

as I stand there next to the little heap
of my Pooh dishes and pencil can

stacked on top of my poetry notebook
and Guernésiais printout.

So she begins to put her things into a pile
A pair of binoculars with a broken strap.

Three plastic plates that once had unicorns
but now the pictures have worn off.

Her favorite too-small green sneakers
with a hole where her big toe poked through.

Sometimes

Sometimes talking is a contest
and the person who talks most wins.

Sometimes silence is a contest
and the person who talks first loses.

Sometimes when you have too much to say,
it's better to say nothing at all.

Sometimes silence is its own way of talking.
Sometimes silence talks louder than talking ever could.

But Sometimes

You can just say two words.
So I say, "Oh, Lizard."

And then she says two words.
"Oh, Bumble."

We reach for each other at the same time,
and we stand there holding on to each other,

both of us crying—I think we're crying—
at least we're crying on the inside,

her tears sloshing around inside of me,
and my tears sloshing around inside of her.

When We Finally Pull Apart

"I wanted to tell you,"
Lizard whispers.

"But I didn't know how.
I had said those horrible things.

I thought you probably hated me.
I sort of hated me, too.

I hoped if I told the others,
they could help me figure out

what to say. But you showed up
before I could finish talking.

And then Zoey told you.
And I never had a chance.

You probably don't believe me.
But it's true, Bumble.

Do you believe me, Bumble?
Please say you believe me.

Bumble?"

I Take a Deep Breath

"I do believe you about my mom,"
I tell Lizard.

Should I say the rest?
Is this the time to say it?

If not now,
then when?

"But I don't believe you
about your dad.

He's not off spying.
He's at home—"

"Drinking,"
Lizard says in a small voice.

"I wanted to tell you that, too.
But I didn't know how

to say that,
either."

Crying

I'm crying on the outside now,
and Lizard is crying, too.

I can feel her wet cheek
pressed against my wet cheek,
so I can't tell which tears are hers
and which are mine.
And I know that instead
of saying good-bye forever,

Lizard and I
are saying

a new and better
kind of

hello.

The Next Day at Lunch

Lizard comes with me to our table.
She lets me do the talking.

"Lizard and I are friends again,
so I want us to sit together the way we used to.

And my mother is home from the hospital,
and she's doing better every day."

There! I said both those things,
and saying them wasn't hard at all.

"Great!" Zoey says.
"I'm glad," Zari says.
"Me, too," Veronica says.

Then Veronica can't contain her big news
any longer.

"You'll never guess who I bumped into
at the grocery store last night
when my mom and I ran in for just a minute
to get throat lozenges because
my vocal cords hurt
from practicing my song so much."

"Who?" I ask to be nice,
because of course I already know the answer.

"Trevor!"

"Trevor?" Lizard asks.

"Trevor!
From the play!
And he tried to act like he didn't see me,
but I know he did because the tips of his ears
turned red in this super-cute way. And then—"

And then Lizard and Zoey and Zari and I
all smile at one another
and let Veronica go on talking.

A Month Later

The play is much scarier
than I thought it would be,
and much more thrilling, too.

You may have heard the expression
"blinded by the light,"
which sounds like a contradiction,

because if you are blind,
your world is dark all the time,
so how can you be *blinded* by *light*?

But it's true.
When the hot, bright theater lights
hanging from the auditorium ceiling

shine straight into your eyes
with their full glaring intensity
for a moment you can't see anything.

You can't see out into the auditorium
where now instead of playing-card boys
horsing around and driving Mr. Delgado crazy,

every seat is filled with parents
and siblings and teachers and friends
who wait in expectant silence

for you to begin your song
and you hope—hope—hope—
you haven't forgotten the words.

Veronica's Big Moment

Before all the flowers sing our song together,
the five real flowers with actual names
have to start speaking their lines.

Lily's one and only line is supposed to be:
"We *can* talk,
when there is anybody worth talking to."
But when Alice says the line
that comes before this,
"Oh, Lily, I *wish* you could talk!"
Lily *doesn't* talk.

Lily doesn't say

anything

at all.

Veronica stands there
rooted to the stage,
as if she were
a *real* flower.

No longer a girl pretending to be a flower,
but a girl who has turned into one
and now can't speak

a single word.

My Big Moment

Standing directly behind her,
I whisper to Veronica,
"We *can* talk!"

She repeats the words
so softly I can hardly hear them,
and she forgets to toss her petals,
and swivel her hips,
and although I can't see her face,
I bet she forgets to roll her eyes
to show her scorn for poor little Alice.

"When there is anybody,"
I whisper next.

"When there is anybody,"
she repeats like a flower puppet.

"Worth talking to."

"Worth talking to."

So don't let anyone tell you
that being an extra flower
isn't an extremely important job.

If you are ever a real flower
and you forget your only line,
hope that you have
a quick-witted extra flower
standing behind you.

At the End of Our Song

The applause is so loud it startles me.
It was such fun belting out our song,
preening and strutting in our mean-flower way,
I almost forget the audience was there.

Now I'm overwhelmed by the clapping
and the whistling and the cheering.

One man is shouting "Bravo!"
and I have a feeling it's my dad,
because that is the kind of
corny,
embarrassing,
but wonderful
thing he would do.

At the final curtain call for the whole play,
the same person who sounds just like my dad
is shouting "Bravo!" again.

In the Lobby Afterward

I find my parents,
who sweep me into a hug.
My dad is holding a huge bouquet of yellow roses,
in honor of my being a yellow rose,
and he's teary-eyed as he gives them to me,
as I knew he would be.

"I'm so proud of you, Betsy!"
my mother says.
She sounds like she means it.
And guess what?
She's teary-eyed, too.

Lizard is there with her mom.
She whispers to me,
"Lily, *can* you talk?
It doesn't sound like you can talk.
Um—Lily—Lily, are you there?"
I burst out laughing,
so I guess the meanness of the mean flowers
is rubbing off on me.
Well, just a little bit.

Mr. Delgado comes up to my dad
and thanks him for his wonderful help
building the backdrop for the flower garden,
with this huge amazing tree
with sheltering, spreading, leafy branches.

Then Lizard goes off to join the crowd around Zari.
The two of them do some stuff together now,
the way that Zoey and I do.
Lizard eats lunch at the Spanish-speaking table
once in a while, too,
because she *is* learning Spanish!
My mother helped her mother
find a terrific after-school class.
I'm not taking it, though,
because I'm taking voice lessons instead.

The best thing?
We get to do another performance
of the play tomorrow night!

My mother and father and Lizard
are going to come to see me again!

Maybe my mother wouldn't call this blooming
(though she had those tears in her eyes as she hugged me).

But I do.

It's a kind of blooming
to lose so much,
even to lose the people you love,
and then find a way to get them back,
different from and better than
how it was before.

It's a kind of blooming
to find the words to say
what you need to say,
and to say them to the people
who need to hear them.

I finally said the words that were in my heart
to my mother and my best friend.

And I'm the one who gets to decide
what blooming means to me.

Author's Note

When I was a child, I read my way through the *Golden Book Encyclopedia*. In the volume for *E* I became entranced by the entry on Esperanto, a language created in the late nineteenth century to be a universal language that could be shared by speakers all over the world. How wonderful it would be, I thought, if everyone in the world could speak the same language! I was wild to find a way that I could start learning Esperanto myself.

As the years went by, however, I began to appreciate the amazing diversity of the world's languages; I no longer valued the search for one single language that everyone in the world could speak. When I learned that the earth's treasury of languages was becoming increasingly endangered by the forces of globalization, I thought how I would have felt if I had known this as a child. Just as, decades ago, I had wanted to learn Esperanto to promote universal understanding, now I would have wanted to learn an endangered language to save it from utter extinction. This was the seed from which this book grew.

I began my research by reading *Dying Words: Endangered Languages and What They Have to Tell Us* by Nicholas Evans, who studies Australian Aboriginal languages at Australian National University. The website Lizard and Betsy first discover in their internet searching is loosely based on the website for the Endangered Languages Project: www.endangeredlanguages.com. This website lists (at the time of this writing) 166 endangered languages within the United States alone, all languages of First Americans threatened by centuries of conquest and deliberate efforts on the part of the U.S. government and other institutions to exterminate Indigenous cultures and especially Indigenous languages.

The language videos the girls listen to are inspired by the "Conversations in Guernésiais" videos available on You Tube: www.youtube.com/playlist?list=PLucc9aUimz0mhgn5RvNI hOv3q3-L8Bj-A, although I did not follow the conversations in the videos exactly. The written resources the girls find are drawn from a variety of online sources. It is not easy to find good online sources for learning endangered languages, so I somewhat simplified the search Betsy and Lizard would have had to go through to find helpful language-learning tools for Guernésiais.

Statistics on the number of speakers for any language are impossible to compile with precision and change constantly. For Guernésiais, I saw numbers ranging from two hundred to three hundred remaining speakers and chose two hundred for simplicity. Most endangered languages—including Guernésiais—have variations in how they are represented in written form, so there may be no one correct answer for how to write down any words in Guernésiais, or how best to give a phonetic rendering of it.

One of my hopes in writing this book was to call attention to the amazing linguistic wealth of our world and the dangers facing it. My goal has been to foster appreciation of the many different ways in which human beings talk to one another—diversity that may someday, tragically, vanish forever.

Acknowledgments

This is a book about language. It's a book about finding the words that let us say what we most need to say. For me, right now, this means finding the words to say thank you.

To the writer friends who read the earliest draft (Tracy Abell, Vanessa Appleby, Jennifer Bertman, Laura Perdew, and Jennifer Sims), thank you for your brilliant insights tempered with kindness toward me at this most vulnerable stage in the writing process. Leslie O'Kane, thank you for letting me know when this was ready to share with the larger world.

To my agent, Steve Fraser, who is always the most encouraging agent on the planet, thank you for being extra-encouraging this time and shouting your love for the book from the rooftops.

To my extraordinary editor, Margaret Ferguson, thank you for believing in this book enough to make me work harder than I've ever worked before, until I had finally wrung out onto the page (in those *four* rounds of revision!) everything that was in my heart.

To my sharp-eyed copyeditor, Janet Renard, thank you for finding whatever Margaret and I had missed with loving attention to every single word.

To Kathrin Honesta, who produced a cover so beautiful, and so perfectly capturing the spirit of the book, that it thrills me every time I look at it.

To the Holiday House art director, Kerry Martin, thank you for making the appearance of the book worthy of what I tried so hard to do with its content.

Finally, to Susan Campbell Bartoletti, Lisa Rowe Fraustino, and Molly Fisk, thank you for bringing poetry back into my life and helping me to develop my own poetic voice. This book would not exist if it hadn't been for that decade of poetry retreats, held first at a country inn in Pennsylvania, and then at a convent in New Jersey. I will never be able to find the words to thank you adequately for sharing the joy of poetry with me, all three of you, in so many ways, for so many years.